What a d...

In all that had happened, one image rose above them all.

Gabe McGregor. Tall, broad shouldered and with eyes that could light the sky. The strength of his arms around her went a long way toward restoring her faith in humanity.

Kayla relaxed against the porcelain tub.

A noise from the other room startled her. She reached for her radio, turning the music off. Silence filled the room, the only sound that of her breathing and the thunder of her pulse against her eardrums.

"I'm hearing things," Kayla said out loud and sank back into the warmth of the bathwater.

A scratchy, tapping sound brought her out of the tub. Her wet feet slipped on the smooth tile and she grabbed for the sink to steady herself. She glanced at the mirror, the steam from the bath having fogged her reflection. Bold letters glared at her, clinging to the glass where the mist dripped free.

SCARED?

★ ★ ★

Dear Reader,

I had fun writing a book with a teenage character in it. My last teenager has graduated from high school and is now in college. Living through her drama reminded me of my teenage years and how I wanted only to fit in and be appreciated and loved by my friends and family.

I was fortunate to have caring parents who didn't quite understand the new generation, but never stopped loving me no matter how difficult I made their lives.

This story is set on the west coast in Oregon where mists rise from the sea like a Devil's Shroud, hiding sins of the evil from those who just want to live a peaceful existence.

Gabe McGregor is struggling to understand a teenage son he never knew until recently, while protecting the new girl in town, artist Kayla Davies, from a serial killer.

Watch as Kayla, Gabe and Gabe's son learn from each other and open their hearts to a love that will bring them together as a family.

Happy reading!

Elle James

ELLE JAMES

Deadly Reckoning

ROMANTIC
SUSPENSE

Recycling programs
for this product may
not exist in your area.

ISBN-13: 978-0-373-27768-1

DEADLY RECKONING

Copyright © 2012 by Mary Jernigan

This edition published by arrangement with Harlequin Books S.A.

For questions and comments about the quality of this book please contact us at Customer_eCare@Harlequin.ca.

® and TM are trademarks of Harlequin Books S.A., used under license. Trademarks indicated with ® are registered in the United States Patent and Trademark Office, the Canadian Trade Marks Office and in other countries.

www.Harlequin.com

Printed in U.S.A.

Books by Elle James

Harlequin Romantic Suspense

Deadly Reckoning #1698

Harlequin Intrigue

Other titles by this author available in ebook format.

ELLE JAMES

A Golden Heart winner for Best Paranormal Romance in 2004, Elle James started writing when her sister issued a Y2K challenge to write a romance novel. She managed a full-time job, raised three wonderful children and she and her husband even tried their hands at ranching exotic birds (ostriches, emus and rheas) in the Texas Hill Country. Ask her, and she'll tell you what it's like to go toe-to-toe with an angry 350-pound bird! After leaving her successful career in information technology management, Elle is now pursuing her writing full-time. She loves building exciting stories about heroes, heroines, romance and passion. Elle loves to hear from fans. You can contact her at ellejames@earthlink.net or visit her website at www.ellejames.com.

This book is dedicated to my editors Elizabeth Mazer and Patience Bloom, who saw something worth printing in my writing and who guided me in producing a much better book.

Chapter 1

"Good night, Kayla. Get some rest, you deserve it." Brent Kitchens, the owner of the most prestigious art gallery in Seattle, escorted Kayla to the side exit of the gallery where she'd parked her car earlier that day. "Thanks for the great turnout."

"The thanks goes to you, Brent." She smiled at Brent, twisting the shiny gold locket at the end of a fine chain that hung around her neck. "I'm headed for my apartment and bed. These things exhaust me." That and being three months pregnant, a secret she hadn't shared with anyone. She wasn't certain how the news would impact her exploding career as an artist, especially since she planned to raise the child on her own.

"Get some rest, sweetheart." Brent patted her back. "Want me to have security walk you out?"

"No, I'll be fine. Thanks again." Kayla kissed the man on the cheek and left the building. The click of the door closing behind her made her jump and hurry toward her car. Having arrived during the day, she hadn't realized how little lighting there was at the back of the gallery. The one light shining out over the cars barely reached hers, casting more shadows than light on her solid black SUV. Keys in hand, she hit the automatic door locks as she neared the rear of her vehicle. When she reached for the door handle, she noticed movement out of the corner of her eye.

Before she could react, a hand clamped over her mouth, stifling her scream and cutting off her air.

Kayla kicked and fought, her desire to live and protect her baby giving her sufficient motivation, but she was overpowered by her attacker's strength. She kicked out, her arms and legs flailing, her hands on her keys desperately fumbling for the little red panic button that she'd never before used.

The man slammed her into the side of the car.

Pain shot through her ribs, and she feared for the fetus growing inside her, but she couldn't escape the hold. Then she was flipped around, pinned to the car with the weight of his body, one hand covering her mouth, the other hand holding an arm. She faced a man with no face, his entire head covered in a ski mask, his eyes the only feature visible in the limited lighting. Light brownish eyes, almost gold, like those of a lion, if the lights weren't playing tricks on her fear-filled mind.

He laughed.

The low rumbling sound sent a ball of lead to the pit of Kayla's stomach. The man hadn't made a threat, hadn't said a word, but Kayla knew without a doubt that he'd kill her. With her free hand, she desperately pressed the buttons on the key chain, struggling to find the right one. The door locks clicked on and off, the lights blinking.

Her attacker's eyes narrowed and he grabbed for her hand and the keys she held.

Kayla finally found the panic button and she hit it just as a hand closed over the wad of keys.

The horn blared, over and over, the headlights and taillights blinking in unison, filled the parking lot with noise and light.

She couldn't see it, but she heard the creaking hinges of the back door to the gallery opening. If she wanted to live, she had to get help. Now!

Kayla bit down hard on the hand over her mouth.

The man cursed, his hand moving just enough that Kayla could let out a short, loud scream.

"What the hell?" Brent's voice called out. "What's going on out there? Hey, someone call 911!" he shouted. "Kayla? Kayla, is that you?"

In a flash, the man moved his grip to her throat, squeezing so hard, Kayla couldn't breathe.

She pried at his hands, her fingers tearing at his flesh, frantic to take a breath.

As his fingers tightened on her neck, he leaned close until his mask-covered mouth was close to her ear. "You win for now, but it isn't over." He yanked the chain from around her neck, then he let go so suddenly, Kayla slid down the side of the car. Unable to slow her fall, her head hit the pavement with a dull thud.

Dense fog clouded her vision even as precious air filled her starving lungs. Muffled voices, like people shouting into pillows, faded into silence. She could see the silhouette of her attacker sliding away into the shadows of an alley. Then the flashing stopped and night turned to pitch, the fog all-consuming. She couldn't let it claim her.

Kayla's eyes opened and she stared at the light shining on her table beside the bed. As quickly as the dreams came to her, they receded. The only impression she retained was one of terror and golden-brown eyes.

She jerked up out of the bed, her breathing labored as if she'd been smothered. Air, she had to get air. Kayla rushed for the window, pushing aside the drapes. She unlatched the lever and shoved the window open, sucking in air as fast as her lungs could take it.

Finally, her heart rate started to slow, and reason took hold once more. She reminded herself that she was far away from Seattle, safely tucked away in her vacation rental in Cape Churn.

Getting away had been her therapist's idea, but the small, seaside town she'd chosen as her destination had been a whim, the result of a real-estate brochure that had caught her eye. The images of untamed waves, peaceful beaches and quaint, quiet streets had called to her in a way she couldn't explain. It just looked like such a *wholesome* place to be. A good place to rediscover her inspiration again—missing ever since the attack. "A good place to have a child," she whispered.

She rubbed her hand in gentle circles over her belly. It was too soon to feel the baby yet, but she liked to imagine her kicking back in reply. Her baby—the only person she had left in the world. When she'd woken up in the hospital after the attack, the doctor had told her she was lucky she hadn't miscarried. If she wanted to keep the baby, she'd have to take better care of herself, get more rest and not worry so much. And stay away from dark places where bad guys hang out.

The doctor had also asked some pointed questions about her support network—family, friends, the baby's father—and hadn't seemed too pleased with the answers. Kayla didn't blame him. As much as she'd hated to admit, she didn't have a support network. Kayla didn't have siblings or parents to call and check up on her. Her best friend and the surrogate father of her baby had died three months ago in a car accident. The crash had occurred only two days following the artificial insemination of Tony's sperm.

For all the years she'd been on her own since the deaths of her parents, she'd longed for a family. She and Tony hadn't been in love, but they had cared for each other deeply, and they'd looked forward to making a family together, raising their child as partners in a home full of warmth and caring—a place where Kayla could finally feel as if she belonged.

"We'll still have that, Baby. I'm sorry you won't have a daddy, but you'll always have me, and we'll be okay."

Thoughts of her baby had gotten her through the loss of her best friend and the end of their plans to build a happy, companionable little family together. Remembering her baby had given her the strength to fight off her attacker in the parking lot long enough to signal for help. And it was with the goal of protecting her baby that she'd grimly pulled herself together in the aftermath of the attack and found a place where they could be safe.

Kayla peered out the window. Fog had crept in to cloak the coastline. If not for the gentle splash of waves against the cliffs and the strong scent of salt in the air, she wouldn't have known that she was at the coast. Her heartbeat settled into a smooth, steady rhythm, as the last vestiges of the nightmare slowly slipped away.

Sleep. That's what she and the baby needed. On this quiet edge of coastline, she wanted the peace of the place to wrap around them.

The therapist had taught her this trick of imagining a happy place before she went to bed. It would help settle her mind and avoid the nightmares that had woken her night after night. Now that she was at Cape Churn, it should be even easier. After all, her happy place was here with the ocean, the wind and waves. The nightmares would fade in time—she had to believe that. She'd get better, stronger. She'd heal in this quiet, peaceful place.

Leaving the window open just a little, she climbed back in bed and laid her head on the pillow.

As she lay there, her eyelids drooped and closed to the darkness, her mind settling into the edge of oblivion. Just as she drifted into sleep, a sharp scream ripped through the night.

Chapter 2

"Found her right there." Judd Strayhorn, one of the local retirees, pointed to where the medical examiner squatted beside the naked body of the dead woman. "I didn't move her. She looked pretty dead already, what with her face buried in sand and her skin all white and waxy-like."

Gabe's gaze raked the beach hoping for clues, articles left behind, footprints, besides Judd's and the medical examiner's. He searched for anything that would tell him how this woman was murdered, who did it and how the body ended up where it did. "Thanks, Judd. If you don't mind coming down to the station later, we can get your statement in writing."

"Anything you want." Judd shook his head, staring across the yellow crime scene tape at the girl's lifeless form. "Hate to think of what the parents of this girl are going to go through. I have a daughter a little older than her." He sighed. "Crying shame." The older man's shoulders sagged as he gathered his fishing pole and tackle box and trudged up the steep hillside to the road.

Gabe couldn't help but empathize. He didn't have a daughter himself but, as he'd only recently learned, he did have a son. Breaking this kind of bad news to parents had always been the hardest part of his job. Now, as a parent himself, Gabe was pretty sure it was about to get harder.

Chief Tom Taggert crossed his arms over his chest. "Think she's the girl from the missing person report last night?"

"Dark red hair, about five foot fourish." Gabe nodded. "Yeah. Got to be the one."

"Her friends said she disappeared from the beach down below the lighthouse round midnight." The chief snorted. "She'd told them she was going to get a blanket from the car."

"Had a high tide last night. Think she waded out and got caught in the undercurrent?" Cape Churn was known for its wicked undercurrent. Not many parents let their small children play in the water near the lighthouse, preferring to take them down the coast to a less dangerous beach. But the teens and young people on vacation at Cape Churn didn't always stop to check the conditions or adhere to the warnings.

"Have to wait for the M.E.'s determination. Can't imagine she'd go in alone, though, and not with the water as cold as it's been."

"Yeah," Gabe agreed. "And if it was an accident, that wouldn't explain why she's naked, when her friends described her as wearing jeans and a hoodie."

The M.E. straightened and walked toward the chief, stepping over the yellow tape. "Tom." He peeled the rubber gloves from his hands and turned to stare down at the victim.

"Gordon." The chief nodded toward the woman's body. "Murder?"

"That would be my bet. I can't say for certain until the autopsy is complete, but there's bruising around her throat. I'll get the report to you ASAP. Until then, I'd be looking for a potential killer."

The M.E. left the chief and Gabe and climbed the steep path behind them.

"I hope you didn't think you'd left the big-city problems behind you in Seattle." The chief stared out at the ocean.

"That's what I was wishing for." Gabe shook his head. "I came home for a quiet, safe place to live."

"We don't always get what we wish for. I told you when you signed on we were normally quiet, but sometimes we have blips on the radar. The blips always seem to come with the fog. You know as well as I do that some of the more superstitious locals call the fog the Devil's Shroud." He shot a glance toward Gabe. "What was the weather like last night?"

"Foggy," Gabe answered, his tone flat, matter-of-fact. He'd almost forgotten the Devil's Shroud tales the old-timers spoke of in whispers as if by speaking of it aloud, the shroud would gain strength.

Tom shook his head. "That damn fog can be a real curse. It can hide a lot of sin."

Gabe couldn't argue with the chief. Fog provided great cover for someone intent on committing a crime. "I'll canvas the area around the lighthouse. Maybe someone saw or heard something."

"You do that. And next time there's a fog, keep your loved ones close. We may have a killer on the loose, and I don't want you taking any chances. You hear me?"

"Yes, sir." Gabe believed in caution—especially with a case as serious as this one. He wasn't naive about small towns, but he really hadn't anticipated a murder in his hometown of Cape Churn. He felt as old as Judd Strayhorn as he ascended the path to the road above and climbed into his cruiser. So much for letting Dakota have free rein on his bicycle. Just because the killer's first target had been a woman didn't mean teenage boys were any safer.

Gabe gritted his teeth. Yet another reason to argue with the teen he still didn't know any better than he did when the boy's mother dropped him off four months ago.

Dakota was testing him, he knew it. What Dakota didn't know was that Gabe didn't give up. And given that Dakota's mother had, Gabe was more determined than ever to make his relationship with his son work. The boy wasn't on his own yet, and he needed to know he had a home to go to, even if he resented the man he refused to call Dad.

Gabe crept along the road headed north toward the lighthouse, stopping at the few vacation cottages and homes along the way. Most remained deserted, the summer season not fully kicked off. Schools in Seattle and Portland were still in session. In Gabe's mind that gave them approximately two weeks to find the killer. After that, they'd have a boatload of potential victims converging on Cape Churn for summer vacation. More people to sift through, and more crime to keep them busy.

With mostly the local population to deal with at this time, how hard could it be to find a killer in a town of less than eight thousand people?

Kayla stood at the edge of the cliff her cottage rested on, her easel propped between the rocks, oil paint stiffening on her palette, a light, cool breeze flipping her hair into her face. She scanned the horizon, hoping for something to catch her eye and spark her inspiration. To her far left, about a half mile away, another jut of rocky cliffs pushed out into the ocean.

Through the trees behind the edge of the cliff loomed the shadowy outline of a building. She couldn't make out much, but Kayla made a mental note to ask Jillian Taylor, the real-estate agent, who lived up there.

But no matter where her gaze fell, nothing grabbed her, and no matter how hard she tried to concentrate, the colors wouldn't take form on the canvas. Last night's scream echoed in her head, over and over. She'd assumed it was a lingering part of her dream. The fog had completely swallowed up her house, she couldn't even see as far as the defunct lighthouse that stood a hundred yards from the cottage.

With conditions like that, if someone truly had been in trouble outside, she couldn't have done anything to help her without risking falling off the cliff.

When Kayla had come out that morning, the sun had burned off the remaining fog and she saw no evidence of a woman, or any of the youths she'd seen yesterday evening, going down to the small stretch of sand below the extremely steep cliffs surrounding the lighthouse.

She'd been too wary to check out the trail they'd used to descend to the beach below. Although her pregnancy wasn't outwardly visible yet, she could feel the changes in her body, the way her center of gravity was shifting. Steep steps on an unfamiliar trail was a risk she wasn't willing to take unless absolutely necessary. Instead, she'd stood at the edge of the cliff and stared down, panning the narrow strip of beach butting up against the rocky cliffs. Nothing stood out. No sign of people. Just nature at its most rugged and beautiful.

The splendor of the rocky coast, the drifting clouds and the steely gray of the ocean called to the artist in her. In a burst of optimism, she'd run back to the house, grabbed her easel, brushes and paints out of the car and hurried back out to paint the edge of the world.

But as soon as she'd taken the brush in her hand, her throat closed up just as it had the night she'd been attacked. Her muse refused to come out of the dark and dance in the daylight.

Kayla stood in the sunshine, her hand holding a paint-brush and a palette filled with blobs of oil paints in varying colors of the earth and sky, and nothing came to her.

Tears filled her eyes and she recognized the new sense of tightening in her throat as the sobs she'd held back since the attack. The fear she'd spent the last two weeks suppressing. It was one thing to be uninspired to paint while she was still in Seattle, with all of its noise, its unfriendly bustle, its shadowed alleyways and crush of strangers. But this was supposed to be a place she could recover, a place to banish her fears and get on with her work. If she couldn't paint here, then that meant there was a chance that the attack outside the gallery had shaken her enough to kill her muse.

Kayla's hands trembled, the tremors jarring the brush from her fingertips. It fell to the rocky ground at her feet.

As she bent to retrieve the brush, a large male hand got to it first.

Kayla screamed and jumped back, the palette filled with paints clattering to the ground. Her hip caught the leg of the easel, jolting it so hard the canvas caught the breeze and flew over the edge of the cliff to crash against the rocks below.

A man leaped forward, yanking her toward him, crushing her against his chest.

Kayla fought him, kicking him in the shins and shoving her hands against his chest.

"What the hell—"

"Let go of me! Let go!" she yelled, landing a solid kick to his ankle.

His grip loosened enough that for a moment, she thought she could back away from him. But he caught her hand, jerking hard, once again slamming her into his solid, muscular chest so hard it took her breath away. This time, before she could punch, scratch or hit him, he clamped her arms against her sides. "Will you be still? I'm not here to hurt you."

"You could have fooled me," she said, barely able to push the words past the fear blocking her vocal cords.

"If I wanted to hurt you, I wouldn't have grabbed you."

"Huh?" Kayla finally looked up into eyes so blue they rivaled the hues of the morning sky. "You grabbed me so I wouldn't get hurt?"

"You were about to fall over the edge of the cliff." He spun her in his arms, still holding her close.

She faced the edge of the cliff only a foot away.

"When you jumped back, you almost backed off the edge," he said, his breath stirring the tendrils of hair beside her ear.

Rocks slithered over the side, the larger ones pinging against others on their way down to splash into the ocean.

Kayla swallowed hard to keep the bile from rising in her throat. She gulped a lungful of air to settle her stomach. It wasn't until she remembered to breathe that she became aware of the solid wall of muscle pressed against her back and the strong arms circling her waist, keeping her from toppling off the cliff.

"It's a long, bumpy trip down that way." His chest vibrated against her back, sending crazy electrical surges across her nerve endings everywhere his body touched hers, from the backs of her thighs, across her buttocks and around her waist where his arms tightened. The tingling nerves had nothing to do with fear, but something altogether different.

Kayla stiffened. "You can let me go, I'm not suicidal. I won't throw myself over the side, if that's what you're worried about."

His arms loosened slowly, as if he wasn't quite sure whether or not to believe her. He backed away before he let go of her, giving her the space she needed to edge away from the cliff.

She turned and faced the man, her eyes narrowing. Over six feet tall, dressed in a navy-blue uniform, he sported a shiny silver badge on his chest. Broad shoulders filled his navy shirt, the lines tapering to a trim waist and hips.

Kayla inhaled and let out the breath slowly. An officer of the law. Nothing to be afraid of. Other than the way her heartbeat galloped when she stared into his light blue eyes.

Kayla had never seen eyes that blue. His sandy-blond hair ruffled in the wind, giving him a casual, open and appealing look. As if the blue eyes weren't enough, they were accompanied by high cheekbones and a dimple in his left cheek when he smiled, which he was doing now. The effect was to take her breath away, yet again. Out of nervous habit, Kayla's hand reached for the locket she kept hanging from a chain around her neck. Not until her hand met bare skin did she remember that the locket with the picture of her parents had been lost on the night she'd been attacked. She flinched, and pulled her hand away.

"Hi. Gabe McGregor, Cape Churn police officer." He held out a large, calloused hand.

She eased her hand out toward it.

His fingers closed around hers, engulfing them in a warm handshake. It felt good compared to the cool breeze blowing in off the water.

Too good. For two weeks now, she'd had to steel herself to keep from flinching at every man's touch. Her therapist had said it was a perfectly normal reaction to an attack like hers, but it was still unsettling—and part of the reason why she'd chosen such an isolated place to stay. So why did she feel no urgency to get away from Officer McGregor's touch? The lack of fear was odd…and a little disturbing.

"Kayla Davies." She pulled her hand free of his. "Do you always sneak up on people?"

That dimple flashed and Kayla could swear his blue eyes twinkled in the morning sun. "I called out, but I guess you were caught up in what you were doing." His smile twisted. "Sorry about the canvas."

She shrugged. "I hadn't actually put paint to it." She glanced up at him, raising a hand to shield the eastern sun from her eyes. "What brings you out to the lighthouse, Officer McGregor?"

"Call me Gabe." His smile returned briefly before it disappeared and his face grew serious. "I'm here on business."

"Business?"

"Yes, ma'am." He reached into his uniform pocket for a notepad and pen. "Were you anywhere near the lighthouse last night around midnight?"

Kayla looked back at the cottage, her lips curling upward on the corner. "Yes. I'm staying in the cottage beside it. I was in bed trying to sleep. Why?"

He tipped his head to the side. "I didn't know anyone was renting it. How long have you been there?"

"I arrived around dusk last night."

"Did you notice anyone else out here?"

"Some kids went down a trail to the beach just before dark." She squatted to retrieve the paintbrush that had been forgotten in their earlier struggles and placed it in her work case. "I counted three girls and two boys."

"Anyone else?"

She nodded in the direction of the cliff with the building tucked into the trees. "I thought I saw a man along the cliffs to the south. I think he was walking a dog. I was inside, looking through the window, so I can't be certain. After the sun set, I closed the blinds on that side of the house." She didn't tell him why she'd closed the blinds. He didn't have to know that the new resident of the lighthouse cottage was afraid of the dark.

"What about at midnight? Did you see or hear anything?"

"Like what?"

"Anything out of the ordinary. A car, voices, someone screaming?"

Kayla gasped. "What?" The air around her got warmer, perspiration beading on her forehead.

"Did you hear a car drive up, voices, a scream, anything?"

"Screaming?" Kayla's hand rose to her throat where the air refused to move into her lungs. "Did something happen?"

Officer McGregor's lips pressed into a line. "One of the girls in that group showed up this morning on the beach half a mile away. She'd been murdered."

Chapter 3

Gabe reached out and grabbed for the woman, once again, to keep her from crashing to the ground. She sagged against him, her head lolling back, exposing her neck and the distinct yellowing of fading bruises. What the hell?

"Ms. Davies?" He shifted her, holding her in one arm while smoothing the rich, auburn hair from her eyes. The color of her hair struck a chord with him. Where had he seen dark red hair recently?

Then it dawned on him. The murder victim on the beach had dark red hair. "Ms. Davies, please wake up." He shook her gently.

Kayla blinked, her eyes staring up into his, tears filling them almost immediately. "I'm sorry." She pushed against him, the movement not enough to convince him to let go.

Gabe kept his hold on her, his arm slipping around her waist, her breasts pressed firmly into his chest. He stood a head taller than she did; the soft curls hanging down her back brushed against his hand. Her pale skin against the deep auburn hair gave her a pretty, feminine and fragile appeal that would inspire any man to want to protect her. Including Gabe.

So where did the bruises come from?

"I can stand on my own," she said.

"I don't believe you. If you don't mind, I'd rather hold on until we're well away from the edge of the cliff."

"But I was painting," she said, waving her hand limply.

"Considering the canvas flew over the edge, I'd say you're done for now."

Her gaze held his for a moment, then she sighed. "You're right. Who was I fooling anyway?" The last bit was muttered under her breath.

Keeping one hand around her waist, he handed the box of paintbrushes to her and gathered the easel under his spare arm. "Ready?"

"I guess." She looked at the edge of the cliff where her canvas had gone over.

"Trust me, you won't find it." Gabe urged her toward the cottage. "And if you did, you wouldn't be able to get to it. That part of the bluff is too steep to climb down and back up."

She smiled, a short quirk of her lips. The sun seemed to come out, then fade away as quickly as it rose in her face, her green eyes darkening with her frown. "Really, I can walk on my own."

"Prove it by walking with me first."

She let him walk her several yards away from the edge of the cliff before she glanced up at him. "See?"

Gabe reluctantly let go of her waist, a strange feeling of loss resulting from the separation. He wanted to keep her tucked safely in the crook of his arm. Must be that waif-like appearance she had about her. Her pale skin only emphasized the dark circles beneath her eyes, adding an air of mystery and tragedy to her beautiful features.

They crossed the distance between the cliff and the cottage in silence. Gabe didn't want to start questioning her until he was certain he wouldn't be picking her up off the ground again. A chair would be nice. And apparently, Ms. Davies wasn't anxious to talk right away, either, her lips pressed into a line, the frown furrowing her forehead more worried than angry.

When she reached the cottage and pushed the door open, she paused. "Won't you come in?"

"Thank you, Ms. Davies." Gabe stepped inside and lean d the easel against the wall. The cabin was like so many other cabins along the coast, decorated in light, durable furnishings in keeping with summer vacation beach residences. The open living space had a large picture window facing the ocean.

"Call me Kayla. Ms. Davies makes me sound old." She set the box of supplies on an end table and headed for the kitchen. One after the other, she rummaged through the cabinets, her movements brisk and efficient, but Gabe noticed the way her hands shook a little as she unearthed a teakettle.

Gabe stepped up beside her and grabbed her hands, kettle and all. "Sit." He led her to the dinette table and pulled out a chair, forcing her into it.

For a moment, Kayla looked as if she was about to argue, but then the fight seemed to leach out of her. She stared out the window, her face blank, expression closed. "I thought it was my nightmare."

"What?" Gabe sat across from her and continued to hold her hands in his. "What did you think was your nightmare?"

"The scream." Her gaze shifted from the window to his

face. "I thought it was part of my nightmare. I did nothing."

His stomach did a flip-flop, the desperation in Kayla's face making him want to pull her back into his arms and shield her from whatever ghosts haunted her. He squeezed her hands in his. "So you heard a scream?"

"Yes. I woke from a bad dream and was just going back to sleep when it happened."

"What time?"

"Around midnight. I thought I'd drifted off. I thought the scream was me."

"And what do you think now?"

"I wasn't asleep. I know that now." She dragged her hands from his and buried her face in them. "She screamed and I just lay there."

"You couldn't have known."

When she looked up, he saw that her face was streaked with tears. "I could have helped."

"Or been just another victim."

"If I'd realized what was going on, I could have called the police."

"Likely the man would have gotten away by the time we got there anyway." He took one of her hands in his again. "You didn't kill her. Someone else did."

Her eyes widened and her free hand went to her throat. "H-h-how did she die?"

Gabe's gaze focused on the yellow markings on her neck. "Without having an autopsy report, I can't be certain, but she showed signs of strangulation."

Kayla gasped. "Oh, God, no."

"What?"

"No." She shook her head, more tears slipping down her cheeks before she buried her face in her hands again.

"Kayla, what's wrong?" He reached out to put a hand on her shoulder.

Her body trembled beneath his touch.

"This is my fault."

"What? No, Kayla, I told you. You're not responsible for what the killer has done."

"Yes, I am. You don't understand." She looked up, the expression on her tear-streaked face deadly earnest. "I'm the reason it happened."

Gabe released her shoulder to reach down and take her hand. "Does it have to do with the bruising on your neck?"

She stared up into his face, but there was a vacant look in her eyes that made him uneasy, as if she didn't really see him there. "He followed me, he must have."

"Who followed you?"

"I don't know." Her hand clenched tightly around his. "He's come to kill me. And instead, he's killed that girl, that poor girl...."

"Who, Kayla?" Gabe was filled with confusion. Was someone truly after Kayla? Uneasily, he realized that she did fit the same physical profile as the victim—petite frame and dark red hair. But did that really mean that someone was after her, or was her imagination running out of control? He didn't know her well enough to say.

"Who do you think killed the girl? Who do you believe has come to kill you?" he asked.

"I don't know." She touched the fingers of her free hand to the bruises on her neck. "I just know that he tried to before and almost succeeded."

Some of the blankness faded away. Her green eyes were steady and focused as they stared into his, and she spoke again.

"He's going to try again."

* * *

A few hours later, Kayla was alone in the house again. Officer McGregor had left after he'd gotten the basic story of her attack. He'd promised to contact the Seattle Police Department for the official report in case the incident truly was related to the murder of the girl on the beach, but he had assured her that a connection was unlikely.

Cape Churn was a three-hour drive from Seattle, and by her own report, hardly anyone in Seattle knew where she had gone. The odds were very slim that her attacker would know how to find her. And yet, as Kayla stood barefoot at the window overlooking the road, she felt like a bird trapped in a gilded cage.

The scenery out the front of the cottage wasn't quite as picturesque as out the back overlooking the ocean, but she could see when people drove up or passed by on the road.

For now, the ocean view had lost its appeal. Her easel stood beside the back window, the view as glorious as the day before, the sun high in the sky, casting brilliant light over rocky cliffs and steely gray water speckled with white-capped waves. But Kayla couldn't find the right colors on her palette to start, an image of a body floating in the current swimming through her mind, taking away from all the glory of nature.

A woman had died pretty much outside her cottage the night before and she had heard her cry for help.

She couldn't stop thinking about what would have happened to her if someone had not heard her cries for help back in Seattle. What if her attacker had finished her off, taking her life—and her baby's life—the way someone had taken the life of the woman found on the beach?

"I messed up, Baby," she murmured. "Maybe I could have helped that girl if I'd just realized…" She squeezed shut her eyes, pain twisting in her gut. "I let her down, and I'm so afraid of letting you down, too."

She reached down to stroke her belly. "This place was supposed to be safe, a place where no one could hurt either of us, but now I'm not so sure. The worst part is that I just don't know where that place would be."

Her stomach rumbled, serving as a reminder to save her introspection until later and get to work on eating for two right now.

As she rattled around in the kitchen, she forced herself to concentrate on the task at hand. She couldn't let herself dwell on her fears. It wouldn't accomplish anything. Officer McGregor was probably right, anyway, that the attack was in no way related to hers. It was a tragedy—a horrible, senseless tragedy—but it wasn't her fault. It had nothing to do with her at all.

So why couldn't she believe that?

On the other side of town, Gabe McGregor pulled his police cruiser up next to the teenager walking his bicycle, slid the passenger-seat window down and leaned over so that he could see the boy's face. "I've been looking all over for you. Where were you?"

The teen shrugged. "Around." He pushed his bike up one of the many hills surrounding Cape Churn.

Gabe kept pace, while tamping down his frustration. "We've been over this before. I don't mind if you visit your friends, I'd just like to know when you do, where you're going and when you're headed home."

"Kinda stalker-like, if you ask me."

"Not the way I look at it." Talking through the open window wasn't any way to get through to a troubled teen. Gabe pulled ahead of Dakota and parked on the side of the road, blocking the boy's path. He climbed out, smiled and waved at a passing car before resuming his conversation with the stranger who was his son.

He'd known about Dakota for only a matter of months. The boy's mother hadn't bothered to tell him that a son had resulted from his brief fling with the older woman back when Gabe was a teen. Siena had been twenty-five, Gabe had been a naive eighteen-year-old, flattered by an older woman's attentions. He'd even imagined himself in love with her. She'd been on vacation with friends at Cape Churn. When she'd left, he hadn't heard from her again, until four months ago.

Siena had shown up at Gabe's apartment in Seattle long enough to tell him that he had a son. She'd pushed the boy carrying a single suitcase in front of her, stating she couldn't handle him anymore. Then she'd left.

After the initial shock wore off, he realized he couldn't raise a kid in downtown Seattle, especially not with the crazy hours he kept serving on the Seattle police force. He quit his job and moved home to Cape Churn. But nothing had prepared him for the difficulties of raising a teenage boy—a troubled one, at that. Apparently Dakota had gotten into a little legal trouble. It was nothing too serious, but he was on probation, and that had apparently been the straw that had broken the camel's back when it came to Siena's patience with their son.

Gabe pushed his hand through his hair, rather than pulling it out, and stood in front of Dakota. He needed instant dad lessons. "I don't ask you to keep me informed because I want to stalk you. I ask you because I care."

"Could you care a little less? I'm not a baby. I don't need a keeper." The words he didn't say, but Gabe felt, were *I don't need you.*

He let the implied meaning slide off his back. Whether or not Dakota thought he needed his father, he needed someone. And since Gabe was the only one he had, Dakota was stuck with him until he finished high school. Gabe didn't give up easily. "No, I can't care a little less. You're my son."

Dakota snorted.

Gabe's lips pressed together to keep from saying something about the boy's attitude. He remembered having a similar one when he was Dakota's age. Thank goodness his parents hadn't given up on him. "As I've told you before, I didn't know about you until recently, or I would have been more involved as a parent all along. But I know about you now—you're here, I care and we're going to figure out this father-son thing if it kills us."

Okay, so that wasn't quite what he'd meant to say, but so be it. He'd tried all the textbook suggestions on getting through to a teen and they had worked no better.

"I want to know where you go so that I know you're safe."

"Really?" Dakota's brows rose into the shaggy hair hanging down over his brow. "Like, this town has nothing goin' on. Why wouldn't I be safe?"

Gabe sucked in a deep breath, last night's victim surfacing much too quickly. "I take it you haven't heard."

"Heard what?"

"About the woman found strangled on the beach this morning."

That got his son's attention. Dakota stared up at Gabe, his eyes narrowing. "You're not pullin' my leg just to get me to call, are you?"

Gabe's lips pressed together into a thin line. "Wish I was."

Dakota's face paled. "Dead? Really?"

"Yeah. I don't like you being out on these roads alone."

The teen's brows scrunched together, that rebellious look returning. "I'm not a girl. I can take care of myself."

"Are you sure?" Gabe asked. "Women aren't the only murder victims in the world, you know."

"So, that doesn't mean it'll happen to me." His son bounced the bicycle impatiently. "Is that all you wanted?"

"Let me know where you're going and when. That's all I'm asking. That way I'll know which ditches to look in if you don't come home on time."

"You wouldn't have to worry about me being run off the road if I could drive myself."

"Boy, you are so wrong." Gabe shook his head, a smile curving his lips. "When you start driving, I'll worry even more."

"Not like I'll be driving anytime soon." Dakota sighed.

"Your probation ends on Saturday. We'll start driving lessons then, I promise."

Dakota scuffed his tennis shoe against the gravel on the shoulder of the road. "Stupid to be on probation for a little graffiti."

"It's considered destruction of property," Gabe stated in a matter-of-fact way. "Property that doesn't belong to you. How would you feel if someone painted your house with graffiti?"

"I wouldn't know. I don't have a house."

Gabe sucked in a deep breath and let it out. The kid had a point. They were living with Gabe's sister in her bed-and-breakfast until Gabe found a house he liked enough to buy. "Just call and leave a message on my voice mail when you come and go from your friends' houses, will ya?"

"I don't have any friends."

"At least text me to let me know where you're going." His voice was a little sharper than he'd intended, but he couldn't walk on eggshells with the boy forever. "And don't be late for dinner, it makes your aunt crazy."

Gabe climbed back into the cruiser and pulled out onto the road, his gaze shifting between what was in front of him and the boy in the rearview mirror. He didn't like leaving him on the side of the road, but short of manhandling him into the cruiser, he had no other choice. The kid just didn't get it.

A murderer was loose in Cape Churn. Until they caught him, no one was safe. The knot in his gut tightened. Though he'd assured her otherwise, Gabe had begun to wonder if Kayla's attack was connected.

Chapter 4

Kayla woke from a nap on the couch, surprised she'd fallen asleep at all. Drawn to the picture window overlooking the ocean and the road leading up from town, she noted the sun hovering over the horizon. It would be dark soon. A shiver of dread slithered down her spine.

A movement out of the corner of her eye caught her attention. Kayla's heart skipped a beat and then thudded against her chest. Her hand rose to her throat where her breath lodged, as a solitary figure appeared walking along the road. At first all she could see was a dark silhouette, until the figure moved closer.

Finally, Kayla could make out a teenage boy pushing a bicycle.

She let go of the breath caught in her throat and laughed shakily. She really was a mess. "Your mommy's losing her mind, Baby. But don't worry, I have six months to get it back before I can start driving you crazy, too."

Maybe coming to the coast wasn't such a good idea. Alone on the edge of a cliff almost made her feel more of a target than if she'd been surrounded by people in a bustling city.

The boy stopped, dropped down by the rear wheel of his bicycle, fiddled with something and then stood, his gaze panning the area.

When he spotted the cottage, he resumed pushing the bike. Instead of passing by on the road, he turned onto the gravel drive leading down to the lighthouse cottage.

Moments later, the teen knocked on the door, the sound jolting Kayla from her stupor. When she didn't move to open the door, the boy leaned to the side and peered into the window. He blinked and stepped closer, his hand cupping around his eyes and pressing against the glass. "Hello?" The teenager's gaze landed on her and his face brightened. "Miss, could I use your telephone?" he called out, his voice muffled by the thick panes of glass.

It would be rude to ignore the boy. "Is everything all right?" she asked, her voice little more than a squeak. Oh, no, what if someone else had been hurt? Had another woman been attacked?

"I got a flat tire on my bike. I need to call the police station."

"The police?" Kayla inched toward the door. "Why the police?"

"Why not?" He shrugged. "It might give them something to do."

Something to do? Kayla shook her head. Had the boy not heard about the murder? Curiosity warred with wariness, pushing it to the side. The teen looked harmless enough. A glance at his bicycle confirmed the flat tire. He was as tall as she was and lanky, but not very muscular. Certainly not big enough to overpower a woman and strangle her to death. And surely he wasn't the man in Seattle two weeks ago who had tried to kill her. The boy didn't have the build. What did Kayla have to worry about?

"Just a minute." Kayla left the chain secure over the door, while she unlocked the doorknob and the dead bolt. She eased the door open and stared out at the young man. "I'm not sure the landline's been turned on yet. Give me a minute, will you?"

"Sure. I guess I could push the bike all the way to the B and B, but the old man will go ballistic if I'm late. Thinks I'm a little kid or something." The boy turned his back to the door and scuffed his tennis shoe against a porch column. "This place is so dead, it's lame."

Kayla cringed at the young man's choice of words and closed the door, racing for the telephone on the kitchen counter. She lifted the receiver. No dial tone. With a sigh, she replaced the phone on the charging unit and dug in her handbag for her cell phone. The display showed two bars. Maybe.

Back at the door, she unlatched the chain and handed the phone to the kid. "The landline isn't connected yet. But you can try using my cell phone. No guarantees—the reception isn't great. But I got a call through yesterday."

The boy punched in the numbers and hit the send key. After a few moments, he shook his head. "Nothing." He pressed the redial key and waited again. With the same response, he closed the phone and handed it back to Kayla. "Guess I'm walking. Thanks anyway." He turned and stepped off the porch.

Kayla watched him amble down the gravel road, shoulders slumped. She called herself every kind of fool. If she let herself be afraid to step out of the house, she'd more or less create her own prison. That was no way to live. If she retreated from life in fear, her attacker back in Seattle had won.

Bull on that!

Kayla was made of sterner stuff. Officer McGregor was right. Her attack had nothing to do with the woman killed last night. No one knew where she'd gone. She'd told no one. He couldn't have followed her.

Guilt and determination pushed her out the door to stand on the porch. "Wait!" she called out. "I have an SUV. I'm sure I can fit the bicycle in the back. Want a lift?"

He turned, shielded his eyes from the sun falling toward the sea. "No, thank you. I don't want to bother you."

"I insist. Just give me a minute to get some shoes on." When she turned to close and lock the door, she stopped herself. The boy wasn't going to bother her, and she'd be damned if she acted like a pathetic old lady, locking herself inside every minute of the day. She purposely left the door unlocked and opened as she ran for her room to dig out her sandals.

When she returned to the living room, she gasped.

The teen stood beside her easel, holding up the palette and paintbrushes. When he heard her gasp, he dropped the items to the table beside the easel. "I'm sorry, the door was open. I thought you wanted me to come in."

Kayla laughed, her voice shaky. "I did want you to come in," she lied. "I just didn't expect you to be so quick."

"A guy would be stupid to pass up a free ride." He nodded at the easel. "You paint?" He snorted. "Dumb question. Of course you do, why else have paintbrushes and an easel?"

Kayla stared at the empty canvas and sighed. "I used to paint."

"Used to paint?"

She shrugged and gathered her keys from the kitchen

countertop. "Haven't felt much like it lately." Hooking her purse over her shoulder, she stared across at the boy.

He didn't seem at all in a hurry, intent on studying the paints, pressing his finger to the globs of oil on the palette. "I like the way the colors blend and make new colors."

"Me too. It's one of the reasons I took up painting in the first place." Kayla moved closer to where the boy stood. "Seeing as I'm giving you a ride home, it might be nice to know your name."

"Dakota." He glanced at her. "Are you any good?"

"At driving?"

"No, painting."

Kayla almost laughed out loud. She never took her talent for granted, nor her success over the past five years. From selling her paintings on the sidewalks of Seattle to being sought out by rich-and-famous art aficionados, she'd come a long way. Good at it? The laughter died before it could emerge. "Sometimes."

The teen turned away from the palette, the canvas and the brushes and strode to the door. "At least you don't get fined, put on probation and kicked out of your home for your art." He pushed through the door and jumped off the steps to the ground below.

"Fined?" Kayla followed him out, locking the door behind her.

When he didn't respond, she didn't push. She wanted to ask him what he meant, but the stormy look on his face didn't invite confidences.

With a tap on her key fob, she popped the latch on her SUV and the back door rose. The backseats were still folded down from when she'd loaded all her suitcases and art supplies for the trip south from Seattle.

Between the two of them they managed to get the bicycle in place, laying it on its side. Kayla let Dakota handle the heavy lifting. Once it was inside, Dakota climbed into the passenger seat while Kayla closed the hatch and rounded the vehicle to the driver's side.

As she settled behind the steering wheel, the sun glinted off something shiny, blinding her for a moment. That something dangled off the rearview mirror. She blinked and held up her hand to keep from being flashed again. She touched a thin chain, her fingers curling around it. When she looked down, her heart stopped, her breath lodging in her throat. In her palm lay a golden locket—the locket she'd worn the night of the art show in Seattle. The night she'd almost lost her baby. The night she'd almost been murdered.

Gabe stepped out of the shower, grabbed a towel and scrubbed the water from his hair, his thoughts poring over the events of the day, the murder weighing heavily on him.

He'd been with the sheriff when they'd given the young woman's parents the news. His chest was still tight from witnessing their disbelief and then the overwhelming grief in their eyes.

Adding to his crapper of a day, Dakota hadn't been home when he'd gotten off work. Another ten minutes and he'd be late for dinner.

Not that Gabe cared so much about punctuality. He worried where the boy was and whether or not he was in any kind of trouble.

The front door opened and closed on the big old house.

Gabe looped the towel around his neck, slipped into a pair of jeans and padded barefoot through the bedroom door and out onto the landing overlooking the large foyer. "Dakota?"

When no one answered, he hurried down the stairs, reaching the bottom just as the door opened again and

Kayla Davies entered, followed by Gabe's sister, Molly, with Dakota bringing up the rear.

Kayla stopped so suddenly that Molly ran into her back, bumping her forward and into Gabe's bare chest.

His hands automatically rose to steady her, a smile quirking at the corners of his mouth. "Hello, again."

She stared up at him with deep green eyes, her hands resting against his bare skin.

"Oh, I'm sorry," Molly said. "I was too busy looking down I didn't see you stop. Hi, Gabe, meet our new neighbor, Kayla." Her brows rose. "You might want to put a shirt on."

"Yeah, really," Dakota agreed, edging past the women and his father to lope up the steps two at a time, his face a mottled red.

"Wash up, dinner is on in a few minutes," Molly called out to the retreating teen. She shook her head. "I don't know what it's gonna take to get through to him."

Kayla stepped back, twin flags of color rising in her pale cheeks. "Excuse me. I'm not usually so clumsy."

"Blame me." Molly hooked her elbow and dragged her toward the kitchen. "Gabe, get dressed while Kayla and I put the finishing touches on the soup. Oh, by the way, she's staying for dinner."

Kayla glanced over her shoulder at Gabe as Molly pulled her through the swinging door and out of sight.

For a long moment, Gabe stood staring after them, his skin still tingling from where Kayla's hands had rested on his chest. He dragged in a deep breath and let it out, stunned by the impact she had on him. His pulse beat faster than normal, his blood burning through his veins. He'd thought his reaction over their earlier meeting had been one of fear for her life, but this kick in his gut had nothing to do with fear and more to do with physical attraction.

Gabe shook himself, grabbed the towel from around his neck and followed Dakota up the stairs. He needed to remember to keep his head clear. This was no time to get caught up in an untimely attraction. He had too much going on, between trying to connect with his son and finding a killer.

He also had to remind himself that women weren't on top of his most trustworthy list since Siena showed up at his door with a son she'd kept secret from him for years. Growing up in a small town, he'd always assumed that the people he felt close to—family, friends, lovers—were as open and honest with him as he was with them. He couldn't assume that anymore.

He suspected his lack of trust was part of the strain in his relationship with Dakota. He doubted Dakota would feel any better about it if Gabe explained that he was suspicious of everyone, not just teenagers with juvenile court records.

Gabe even had his suspicions that Kayla was keeping something from him. He wanted to know everything he could about this stranger with the porcelain skin and long silky hair. But the timing was all wrong—not least because he was afraid she might be in danger.

He'd spoken to the detective on her case back in Seattle. It sounded bad. Very bad. It obviously hadn't been just a random attack. There had been phone calls leading up to it—threats, harassment. And then, on the night at the gallery, the attacker had told her that it wasn't over.

No, this definitely wasn't a time when either one of them needed the distraction of a relationship.

Three minutes later, he stepped out onto the landing,

securing the buttons on a crisp white dress shirt, his hair combed back, shoes on his feet.

Well, just because he wasn't looking for a relationship was no reason not to look his best.

He'd stopped to knock on Dakota's door. "Ready?"

"I'll be down in a minute," the teen muttered, the steady *thump, thump* of music carrying through the wood paneling.

Gabe descended to the ground floor and headed straight for the kitchen, where he found Molly pouring a stockpot full of clam chowder into two large soup tureens.

"Hold that, will ya?" She handed him the stockpot, hot pads and all, and scraped the last drops of soup into the serving dish.

"That's an awful lot of soup for the four of us."

"We have additional guests coming for dinner."

Gabe's gaze drifted around the kitchen.

A smirk lifted one corner of his sister's mouth. "She's out on the porch, taking in the sunset."

"Who?"

Molly shook her head. "Don't play dumb with me. You had your hands on her long enough to grow roots."

Heat rose around Gabe's collar. His sister knew him all too well. Probably better than he knew himself. "She stumbled."

"Yeah, but you held on—never mind." Molly took the stockpot from him and plunked it into the sink. "Tell me all, and make it fast, I have to get this on the table before the guests start bellyachin'."

Gabe stiffened. "There's nothing to tell." And, really, there wasn't, just a feeling. He barely knew the woman.

Molly snorted. "Bull."

Gabe refused to elaborate. Molly was stubborn, just like their father, but so was Gabe. "How'd she end up here?"

"She brought Dakota home. His bicycle tire is flat. You'll need to help him fix it. Since she was nice enough to bring my nephew home, and I had enough clam chowder to feed an army, I invited her to stay for dinner." His sister grabbed a tureen and backed into the swinging door. "Don't just stand there, bring the other," she commanded.

Gabe grinned, lifted the tureen and carried it into the large dining room where a long table had been set with seating for eight.

"Who do we have joining us?" Gabe asked, not really interested, but stalling for a chance to freely observe Kayla through the window.

"The Johnsons are still with us and while I was in town purchasing supplies, I ran into Jillian and one of her clients. I told them I was making clam chowder and asked if they wanted to come to dinner."

As if on cue, an older couple emerged from the first-floor hallway, hands joined like newlyweds, which they were, having chosen Cape Churn and the McGregor B and B for their honeymoon.

Dakota shuffled down the stairs, headphones jammed in his ears, carrying his iPod, shirt untucked, hair uncombed, the crotch of his jeans drooping nearly to his knees.

Gabe closed his eyes and fought against the urge to tell the young man how to dress. He'd been a teen once. He'd worn weird clothes, listened to his music and basically drove his parents crazy.

He let Dakota's appearance slide, his thoughts shifting to the woman he could see through the front window, leaning on the porch rail, staring out at the steely-blue waters of the cape.

Molly came to stand beside Gabe, wiping her hands on her apron. "We're just waiting on Jillian and her client. Why don't you go talk to our guest. She seemed kind of quiet, and very jumpy. Why, I don't know. I'd try to get her to open up, but I have to get the food on the table. Until Jillian and her client arrive, you have time." Molly's mouth slid sideways. "You know you want to."

Gabe shook his head. Molly's exuberance didn't hide the fact that she was also very intuitive when it came to people and their feelings. She had a way of seeing through him, not that he'd been trying to hide anything.

Kayla Davies intrigued him. He tried to tell himself it was because of her involvement in the murder investigation.

Dakota plopped into an overstuffed leather chair in the sitting room as Gabe passed by, headed for the front door.

When the screen door squeaked, Kayla glanced his way, her green eyes widening for a moment, that haunted look lingering in the shadows beneath her eyes.

"It's beautiful out here," she said, turning her back to him, her gaze skimming across the rugged, rocky coastline.

"I'm kind of partial to it."

Kayla's fingers twisted a strand of long auburn hair, her attention on the view, not him. "Is this your hometown?"

"Yes, ma'am." He leaned against one of the wide columns and stared at her rather than the scenery. "Lived here most of my life except the time I spent as a Seattle street cop."

"Seattle?" Her gaze shot to him.

"Hard to picture me fighting crime in the big city?"

"No. It's just that we came from the same city." She shrugged. "Just shows you what a small world it is." Kayla glanced out at the sea. "What made you come back to Cape Churn?"

"My son, Dakota."

She spun to face him, her eyes wide. "Your son?"

"You look surprised." Gabe grinned.

"I'm sorry." She glanced down at where her fingers tugged at a loose strand of hair. "I'm so new to town, I didn't know."

"Trust me, you can't be half as surprised as I was when I found out I had a son."

She frowned up at him. "When was that?"

"Four months ago."

Her auburn brows rose up her forehead. "Four months?"

Gabe scrubbed a hand across his short hair. "His mother dumped him at my apartment in Seattle. Before that, I didn't know he existed. Since an apartment's no place to raise a kid, I brought him to my hometown." His lips twisted. "I'm pretty sure he hates Cape Churn. And he's not that fond of me, either. Honestly, other than strange music, I'm not really sure what he likes at all. I'm clueless when it comes to raising teens."

"Can't help you there." Kayla's hand smoothed across her flat stomach. "He seemed really interested in my art."

A chuckle rose from Gabe's throat. "I'm not surprised. He's on probation for defacing private property."

Kayla's head tipped to the side. "He doesn't strike me as someone who'd be deliberately destructive."

"Graffiti."

Her smile, though fleeting, lit her face. "Was it any good?"

Gabe stared at the waiflike woman, hoping her smile would last longer, but her lips tipped downward again, the shadows in her eyes returning.

"From the picture he showed me on his cell phone, yeah." He shook his head. "Not that the courts saw it as anything other than a crime."

"He needs an outlet for his art. One that isn't against the law." Again, that hint of a smile curved her lips.

Gabe's breath caught. He could imagine how much more beautiful she would be with a full smile that reached her deep green eyes. "I brought Dakota here to give him a fresh start." He glanced out across the rough waters of the cape and back to Kayla. "I wonder if it's too small-town for him, though."

"Any place is what you make of it. He could be just as unhappy in Seattle as here."

Intelligent as well as beautiful. Gabe's chest tightened. "So what brought you here? Why did you move into the lighthouse cottage?"

"The attack in Seattle two weeks ago." Her fingers rose to her neck absently, but she grimaced and pulled them away before they touched the skin. "It was too close a call. I couldn't walk down the street without seeing danger in every dark corner."

He tried to suppress the urge to take her into his arms and hold her until her fear faded. After he'd learned what had happened to her in Seattle, he'd no longer been surprised that she'd struggled against him when he'd pulled her away from the cliff's edge. It all made sense.

She fished in her jeans pocket. "He tried to kill me, but he didn't have time. Before he got away, he yanked off the necklace I was wearing." She held up a thin gold chain with a broken clasp and a locket dangling from the middle. "I found this in my car when I got in it to bring Dakota home. It's the same necklace he took that night." Her voice was steady, but he could see the way her hand shook slightly, sending tremors through the necklace chain. "I left Seattle to get away from him. I'm certain now that he followed me here."

Chapter 5

Gabe removed a handkerchief from his back pocket, wrapped the necklace in it and then reached out to take hold of Kayla's hand. She hadn't even realized how cold and shaky she was until the simple touch of his fingers on hers steadied and warmed her. She let him hold her until the trembling subsided. She hadn't felt this safe since before the attack and she didn't want that feeling to stop.

"Why didn't you tell me as soon as you arrived?" he asked, his voice gentle despite the implied scolding in his words.

"You were off duty and I didn't want to frighten Dakota."

"Don't ever hold back on something this important. I don't care if you have to call me in the middle of the night." He released her hand and reached out to take both her arms in his firm grasp as he held her at arm's length. "It might be key to finding whoever murdered the girl on the beach—and keeping him from hurting you again."

Tears slipped from the corner of her eyes, trailing down her cheeks. "So you believe me now—my attack and the girl's death are connected after all. My move to Cape Churn brought a killer here. That girl is dead because of me."

The tension in Gabe's arms increased, as if he was struggling with the urge to pull her close. She was glad he resisted. She didn't know how well she'd react to strong arms trapping her in place, especially now. No matter how comforting holding his hand had felt, surely she'd get that rush of panic if he wrapped his arms around her, wouldn't she?

"No," Gabe replied. "It's like I said before. You did not kill that girl. Some low-life bastard did."

Kayla shook her head. "She wouldn't be dead if he hadn't followed me here."

"You can't think that way. It's not your fault," he repeated, squeezing her upper arms gently.

Kayla gave him a weak smile, then pushed away from his grip. "I'm sorry. I'm such a basket case."

He smoothed the hair from her face and smiled gently. "You must be terrified."

She snorted. "That would be an understatement."

Just then, a car pulled off the highway, the crunch of gravel heralding its approach to the B and B.

Kayla stepped away from Gabe before the driver came within view of the corner of the house where they stood. She turned her back to the oncoming vehicle, scrubbed the tears from her face and wiped her hands on her jeans.

By the time the driver climbed out of the car, Kayla had pulled herself together as best she could.

Gabe turned to greet the new arrival. "Hey, Jillian."

A beautiful blonde stepped out, her feet encased in bright red stilettos, a slim-fitting, gray skirt suit accentuating every curve of her body. She smiled at Gabe and slammed shut the car door. "Gabe, sweetheart. I'm glad you're here. When are you going to take me out on a real date?"

She climbed the steps onto the porch, each foot carefully placed, giving her the appearance of a model on a runway.

"Jillian, you know I love you, just not in that way. You're like a sister to me." When Gabe stuck out a hand for her to shake, she tugged on it, bringing him close to her.

She planted her red-lipsticked lips on his mouth, smacking loudly. "You know you don't mean that." She peered around him at Kayla.

Several inches shorter than Jillian, Kayla stood in a peasant blouse and faded broomstick skirt, feeling as if she blended in with the woodwork next to the more glamorous blonde in her sleek business attire.

"Who've you got here?" The blonde held out her hand, her brows lifting delicately.

"Jillian, Kayla Davies. Kayla, Jillian Taylor."

"What a pleasant surprise." Jillian's lips turned upward in a genuine smile. "Kayla, darling. I stopped by to check on you, but you'd flown the coop. I hope you found everything all right."

Gabe frowned. "You two know each other?"

Jillian hugged Kayla and stood with her arm around Kayla's waist.

Kayla forced a smile to her lips, still shaken by the necklace she'd found in her car and the stab of something smarting like jealousy over Jillian and Gabe's friendly greeting. "Jillian rented the lighthouse cottage to me."

"We've exchanged a number of phone calls and emails, but this is the first time we've actually met face-to-face." Jillian hugged her again. "It's a pleasure." Her smile faded. "I hope you aren't put off by the news this morning. That poor girl, murdered in our town." Her brows dipped low. "But don't you worry. Gabe, here, will find her killer before you know it, won't you, Gabe?"

"I'm working on it." Gabe shoved the handkerchief with the necklace into his pocket, his solemn gaze seeking Kayla's. "I promise to do the best I can to bring him in."

"Please do, I just don't feel safe anymore." Jillian wrapped her slim arms around her middle and shivered.

A lean, black, shiny sedan pulled into the driveway and parked between Kayla's and Jillian's vehicles. A man dressed in tailored slacks and a polo shirt climbed out.

"Lawrence, honey. My directions got you here just fine, didn't they?" Jillian strode toward the man and held out her hand. "Did you check out those properties I listed for you?"

The man climbed the porch steps and took Jillian's out-stretched hand. "I did. I think the one overlooking the bay shows promise. I'm just not certain it has enough acre-age." His gaze slid to Gabe and Kayla, his smile spreading across his face. He nodded at Gabe. "Lawrence Wilson."

"Mr. Wilson," Gabe acknowledged the latest arrival and turned to Kayla. "This is Kayla Davies, Cape Churn's newest resident."

"She's renting the lighthouse cottage I showed you a few days ago." Jillian hooked her arm through Lawrence's and pulled him toward the front door. "I smell Molly's famous clam chowder, let's go inside. We can talk there."

Molly was placing a basket of dinner rolls on the table

when they entered the dining room. "Oh, good. Dinner's ready."

Kayla hung back while the older couple staying at the B and B found seats together. Lawrence Wilson held a chair for Jillian, and Dakota entered, headset still plugged in.

Gabe made a motion with his hand and shook his head at his son.

Dakota frowned, but yanked the earpieces out and slouched into a chair.

Gabe held a chair for Kayla and then sat beside her.

Molly took a seat at the end of the table and smiled at her guests. "If you all don't mind, I'd like to take a moment to say a prayer for the unfortunate girl who lost her life last night."

All heads bowed. Kayla closed her eyes, her fingers clenched around the napkin in her lap.

"Dear Lord, please look out for the young woman whose life was needlessly taken. Help her family through their grief. And Lord, please help the authorities bring the man who committed this heinous crime to swift justice. Amen."

As everyone started talking at once, reaching for food and passing platters, Gabe leaned close to Kayla. "We'll get him."

Kayla stared up into his eyes. "Before he hurts someone else?" she whispered.

"We'll do our best." He reached over and squeezed her hand, then let go as someone passed the basket of rolls to him. "Try these. My sister makes the best honey-yeast rolls on the coast."

Kayla took a deep breath and a roll. She needed something to do with her hands other than twisting them in her lap. And she needed nourishment for her baby.

She could still feel the warmth of Gabe's fingers on

hers. But Gabe couldn't always be there to chase away her fears. Kayla had to deal with them alone.

Molly ladled chowder into a bowl and passed it down the table "So, Kayla, where are you from?"

Kayla placed the bowl of creamy, steaming chowder in front of her, the aroma stirring her hunger to life. "Seattle."

"Are you here just for the summer or do you plan to make Cape Churn your home?"

Kayla smiled. "I'm keeping an open mind." She really didn't want to raise her child in Seattle. Especially not without Tony. No, if she was going to have this child on her own, she'd need the perfect home for the two of them.

"What happened last night isn't making Cape Churn your number-one choice, is it?" Dakota muttered, the first words he'd spoken since taking a seat at the table.

Kayla stared down at her hands in her lap. "I'm so sorry for that girl and her family."

"You think murder and crime is restricted to cities," Mr. Johnson commented, "but it's not." He slathered butter on his roll and bit into it. "Mmm. These are the best dinner rolls I've had in a long time.

"Thanks." Molly tucked her napkin in her lap and reached for one.

Jillian smiled across the table at Kayla. "I'm curious, Kayla. How did you find Cape Churn, and specifically, our little real-estate office?"

Glad the topic had moved off the murder, Kayla answered, "I received a brochure in the mail from your office."

Jillian's brows rose. "Really? Hmm. I don't recall mailing any to Seattle recently. I had planned on doing a mass mailing next week." She shrugged. "Someone must have been reading my mind, and I'm glad they did."

"What is it you do, Ms. Davies?" Lawrence Wilson

lifted a spoonful of chowder to his lips, concentrating on the soup, his gaze never rising to meet hers.

An introvert at heart, Kayla shifted in her seat, aware that all other eyes around the table were directed toward her. "I paint."

"Kayla Davies." Molly's brows dipped. "Seems like I know that name from somewhere. I've been chewing on it, but can't recall."

"She's only the hottest artist in Seattle right now. Heck, probably in the States," Jillian gushed.

"No, that's not it." Molly's eyes widened. "Don't get me wrong. I'm sure you're fabulous, but that's not where I heard your name. I think it was on the news recently."

Mrs. Johnson's eyes widened. "That's right. Weren't you attacked in Seattle a couple weeks ago? It was all over the papers and on television. After an art exhibit or something?"

Kayla's face burned and she tried to think of something to say that didn't sound flippant. All she wanted was for the subject to drop. She'd come to Cape Churn to forget and move on.

"Sure would like more of that chowder," Gabe said, breaking the silence. He handed his empty bowl to Molly. "Saw a vehicle head out to the Stratford mansion. Is Stratford back in town?"

Kayla let go of the breath she'd been holding and tried to relax, grateful that Gabe had deflected attention from her. From beneath her lashes, she darted a glance across the table at Lawrence Wilson.

He'd been staring at her, but as soon as she looked up, his gaze dropped.

A chill cooled the air around Kayla.

Wilson turned to Jillian and asked for the salt and pepper, breaking the tension that perhaps only Kayla felt.

"Nora Taggert said Stratford ordered takeout for two yesterday." Jillian dabbed chowder from her lips. "Wonder who he brought back with him."

"In all the years I've lived in Cape Churn, I don't think I've ever seen him bring someone back to the mansion." Molly poured wine into her glass and set the bottle on the table. "He's such a loner."

Jillian nodded. "Doesn't stay long when he comes. Hard to get to know a man who's never around."

Gabe agreed. He couldn't remember the last time he'd seen Stratford. "How long has he been back?"

"Who knows?" Jillian shrugged. "Nora's mention is the first I'd heard. He hasn't been out and about except to walk along the cliff."

"Never was one to live at the mansion for very long. And when he's there, he doesn't come out. The man's a recluse, if ever there was one." Molly nodded toward Kayla. "He lives on the crag closest to the lighthouse."

"You should see his place." Jillian leaned forward. "It's the biggest house around and practically empty. His grandfather left it to him when he died. As far as I know, Andrew Stratford only comes here to check on the upkeep. Such a shame. I bet I could get a good price for the property."

"Any idea where Stratford lives when he's not at the mansion?" Gabe asked.

Jillian shrugged. "No. He has a service come out from Portland to tend the property and a full-time caretaker we only see on occasion purchasing supplies."

Kayla wondered where Gabe was going with his questions about Stratford. An image of a solitary figure and a silvery-white blur flashed across her thoughts. "Does Mr. Stratford have a dog?"

Molly's brows pinched. "No, that would be Frank Mortimer. Walks his dog along the cliff's edge now and then near sundown. Doesn't like people much."

The man had been walking along the cliff around the same time the group of young people had gone down to the beach below the lighthouse. Chances were, he'd seen them from where he was. "Does Mr. Mortimer leave town much?"

"Hard to say. We really don't see him coming and going. If he does, it's at night when no one is watching."

What if the mysterious Frank Mortimer snuck out at night and drove to Seattle to visit the art galleries after they closed? A tremor shook Kayla.

Gabe made a note to check in on Stratford. His arrival coincided too closely with the death of the girl. Anything different had to be taken into account. He glanced at Jillian's client sitting across the table from him. "How much longer are you going to be in town, Mr. Wilson?"

"As long as it takes." He smiled. "Jillian has been very accommodating, showing me all the prime properties along the coast. I'm sure I'll find what I'm looking for soon."

"Just what are you looking for, Mr. Wilson?" Molly asked.

"Please, call me Lawrence." He held out his bowl. "I'd like more of that wonderful chowder, for one."

"Certainly." She took the bowl from him and ladled more of the aromatic soup into it.

"I'm looking for the perfect place to build a small, exclusive resort that caters to the well-to-do."

"In Cape Churn?" Gabe's brows rose. "I'd think you'd need a whole lot more than a scenic view to lure the rich and famous. We're too rocky and hilly for a golf course and there's limited recreational boating, as the tides are unpredictable, though there are some die-hard divers who wreck dive down below. Only experienced boaters risk getting near the cape."

Wilson smiled, his brown gaze holding Gabe's. "I think Cape Churn has a charm all its own. The solitude and beauty alone would attract the clientele I'm targeting."

Gabe shrugged. "Good luck with that."

"Lawrence was considering the old lighthouse location." Jillian leaned forward, her eyes alight, her enthusiasm infectious. "It's got plenty of land with it for the resort building, the lighthouse itself isn't in bad shape and adds character to the location, and the view is to die for." As soon as the words passed her lips, Jillian clamped her hand over her mouth. "Oh, I'm sorry. I didn't mean it that way. There I go again, putting my foot in my mouth."

Wilson smiled and patted her hand. "And a very pretty foot at that. I haven't settled on the lighthouse location. Don't worry, Miss Davies, although it is beautiful and the cottage is quaint, I'm not sure it meets my needs."

Kayla sighed beside Gabe. "Good. I gave up my apartment lease before moving down. I'm not sure how quickly I could move somewhere else."

The thought of Kayla moving hadn't occurred to Gabe. Now that she'd mentioned it, he wasn't too happy about it. Not that he had any hold on or relationship with the woman. He told himself that he didn't want her back in the city where she'd been attacked. But was she safe here? The return of her missing necklace was an ominous sign. He'd have to talk to her about maybe leaving the lighthouse cottage and moving into town, closer to the police station.

"Oh, Kayla, we hope you don't move away too soon." Molly smiled at her. "I like having long-term neighbors. The summer crowd comes and goes, so it's hard to get attached."

"Thanks." Kayla blushed and smiled. "I'd hoped to stay for a while."

Her smile made Gabe's chest swell. This woman shouldn't have to fear for her life. She should be smiling and laughing.

A surge of protectiveness built inside Gabe, his fists clenching in his lap. Whoever was targeting her had to be stopped.

"Until that property sells," Jillian was saying, "you can stay as long as you like, Kayla. Or you can buy it yourself." She smiled brightly.

"We'll see." Kayla's gaze dropped to her plate.

Gabe could just imagine what her thoughts were on buying a place where a killer might be lurking.

"Kayla, what do you paint?" Molly changed the subject.

"You should see her stuff," Dakota jumped in. "I looked up some of her work online. She's damn good."

"Language," Gabe cautioned Dakota. He made a note to himself to counsel his son on proper table manners and conversation.

Kayla smiled at Dakota. "Thank you, Dakota."

"Dakota paints, too." Molly grinned at her nephew. "He just needs a better venue to do it in. Do you give lessons?"

Dakota's face flamed. "Aunt Molly, she's a professional painter. Why would she want to teach a kid?"

Gabe hid a smile. He'd be damned if the teen wasn't a little smitten with the artist. A glance at the beautiful redhead, and it hit him like a punch in the gut. He was a bit smitten with the woman himself. She had that gentle beauty that made him want to reach out and hold on. But he wouldn't. Couldn't. Not now.

Kayla touched the boy's arm. "No, really, Dakota. I wouldn't mind teaching you. Why don't you come by tomorrow. I can introduce you to something other than the spray paints you've been using."

The boy's eyes widened. "Really?" His brows lowered. "I don't want to interfere with your work, but really?"

"Yes, really," Kayla said. "And you won't be interfering. It'll help me."

Gabe's son frowned. "How so?"

"It'll take my mind of things," she said in a low voice. "So, will you come?"

"Sure." Dakota shrugged, trying to look nonchalant, although Gabe could see a spark of excitement in his blue eyes. "Got nothin' better to do in this podunk town."

Had Gabe been close, he'd have kicked Dakota beneath the table for his ungrateful response to Kayla's offer. He could forgive the teen his rudeness, knowing Kayla wouldn't be alone for at least part of the day and Dakota wouldn't be either.

Gabe's cell phone vibrated on his hip. He checked the caller ID. The station. "Excuse me. I have to take this call." He stepped into the kitchen, out of range of the others at the table. Normally Gabe wouldn't leave the table to answer the phone, but Chief Taggert wouldn't call unless it was important.

He punched the talk button. "McGregor speaking."

"Gabe, got some interesting information from the Seattle police I thought you might want to see."

His pulse leaped. "About the murder?"

"Could be." He paused. "I could use your Seattle cop experience on this one."

His curiosity aroused, Gabe knew what he had to do. "I can be there in ten minutes."

"Do that."

Gabe clicked the off button and strode back into the

dining room. "Sorry to leave you, but duty calls." He grabbed the roll from his plate and headed out the front.

"Gabe," a voice called, and he stopped halfway down the front-porch steps.

He turned to see Kayla in the doorway, her hand resting on the screen, her eyes wide, reflecting a dark shade of forest green. "Is everything all right?"

"I don't know yet."

"It's about the murder, isn't it?"

He thought about lying to keep her from worrying, but realized that no matter what story he told, Kayla Davies wouldn't stop worrying until the killer was caught. "Yes, it's about the murder."

She sighed. "Be careful, will you?"

"Me?" He chuckled and walked back up the steps. "You are the one I'm more concerned about."

She stepped closer to him, her tongue darting out to wet her lips. "Gabe?"

"Yeah?"

"Thanks."

He ached to close the space between them and pull her into his arms, but knew better, letting her have her space. "Tell you what, I'll stop by on my way home and let you know what I find out. I can check your cottage over before you call it a night."

"You'd do that?" She looked up at him, her eyes melting his heart, in spite of all his resolutions to keep his distance.

He nodded, struggling to keep from following through on his raging desire to kiss her. "I'll be there as soon as I can."

She smiled—a warmer, fuller smile than the ones he'd seen on her face up to that point. "Thank you for helping me." Then she turned away and went back inside, the screen door smacking into place.

Gabe got into his SUV and aimed for town, knowing he was headed down a path he wasn't sure he was ready for. Kayla had his insides tied in knots, and her green eyes had burned an indelible impression into his thoughts.

If he wasn't careful, he could fall in love with the red-haired artist with the haunted eyes.

And he knew that it didn't take an artist to know love and murder didn't mix well on any palette.

Chapter 6

Gabe sat in front of the computer screen, staring at the short list of unsolved murder cases, each bearing the same M.O. "Where did you get this?"

"Just for grins, I sent the information about our victim to a buddy of mine in the regional FBI office. He entered the data into their Violent Criminal Apprehension Program database and came up with these cases."

A cold chill slithered down Gabe's spine. Three young women, along the West Coast as far north as Bellingham, Washington, and south to Portland, Oregon, had been murdered. Each woman bore similar features: red hair, green eyes and petite frames. All the women had been strangled within the past six months.

"I called the detective handling the case in Bellingham. He said the killer taunted his victim, building the tension like a cat playing with a mouse."

"Taunted?" Gabe's chest tightened, his heart racing. "How?" His breath caught and held.

"He'd call from blocked numbers and threaten them. Sometimes he left presents for his victims to find. One time, he left a favorite photograph in a victim's car that had been on her desk at her workplace. Another time, he took a ring from a victim's jewelry box and tied it to the chain on the ceiling fan over her bed. It was as if the killer wanted her to be scared, wanted her to fear him."

"Did they call the cops as soon as it started?"

Taggert shook his head. "One did when she found a garden gnome lying in her bed. Her friends said it freaked her out so bad, she couldn't sleep at night."

Just like Kayla. Gabe was reminded of his talk with the Seattle detective. Kayla had gotten similar taunting calls in the weeks leading up to her attack. And now she was getting gifts. A cold lump settled in Gabe's gut. "What did the investigation team do?"

"The usual. Dusted her place for prints. They didn't find any. Asked questions of the neighbors. No one saw anyone coming or going from her house. Questioned relatives and her boyfriend."

Gabe nodded toward the list on the screen. "What of the others?"

"Got off the phone a little while ago with the detective handling the case in Portland. Same thing. Pretty redhead, phone calls, gifts, no clues. All these cases had pretty much gone cold. Nothing to go on."

Running a hand through his hair, Gabe asked the question hanging between them, "Coincidence or have we got a serial killer?"

The chief shrugged. "Hard to say."

"Do we have enough evidence to classify this case as a serial killer? Is it time to turn it over to the FBI?"

"That's what I wanted to talk about."

Gabe stood, crossing his arms over his chest. "Talk."

"Our victim is the same as the others, except one thing." Tom frowned. "He didn't taunt her. I asked her parents if she'd been getting any threatening notes, presents, anything." He shook his head. "Nothing."

"Did you ask her friends?"

He nodded then shook his head. "Nothing. If I call in the FBI, is the case close enough?"

Gabe fished in his pocket and pulled out his handkerchief. "I think we need to call them." Carefully, he unfolded the cloth, revealing the broken necklace Kayla had given him earlier. "And while we're at it, we need to dust this locket and Kayla Davies's car."

"Why?" Chief Taggert squinted at the necklace. "What's this?"

"It belongs to Kayla Davies."

"Is she the artist living in the old lighthouse cottage?"

"Yes, sir." Gabe handed the necklace, kerchief and all, to the chief. "She found it in her car this afternoon. Did you know she'd been attacked in Seattle before she moved here?"

"No. I didn't."

"Apparently it was in the papers and on television." Gabe paced in front of the desk, growing more anxious by the minute. "She was attacked in the parking lot of an art gallery. The man was interrupted before he could finish her off."

"You think it's the same guy?"

"She fits the description. Red hair, green eyes, petite. She'd had untraceable phone calls prior to the attack, threatening her." Gabe nodded at the necklace. "Now this."

"Could be a copycat," Chief Taggert argued.

Gabe planted both hands on the chief's desk. "Not possible. This isn't just any necklace—it's *her* necklace. It was stolen from her by the man who attacked her in Seattle."

"Then why the girl on the beach?"

"Those kids were partying below the lighthouse. The killer could have mistaken the girl for Kayla." Another thought struck him, making his blood run cold. "Or he killed the girl as a message to Ms. Davies."

The chief spun toward his desk and lifted the phone from its cradle. "I'm calling the FBI. You go check on the Davies woman. I don't want another murder on my watch."

Gabe was halfway out the door before the words left the chief's mouth.

Kayla thanked Molly for the meal, arranged for Dakota to come by the following day, bid her farewells and drove to the cottage before the sun completely disappeared below the horizon. She wanted the chance to check it out before dark, to turn on all the lights and inspect all the closets, rooms, cabinets, windows and door locks.

She snorted as she pulled her SUV to a halt in the driveway. "Baby, learn a lesson from this. Don't be paranoid like your mommy. But I guess you won't have to, will you? I'll take care of the paranoia for both of us."

The cottage stood as it had when she'd first arrived. Quaint, with its slate-blue shutters, the white-railed porch and wide picture windows stretching from floor to ceiling, reflecting the sunset like mirrored glass.

For a moment Kayla drank in the beauty of the setting and the sunset, letting a cool waft of salty air drift through the crack in her car window.

She realized she couldn't stay in her vehicle forever. Nor could she wait for who knew how long for Gabe to show up and chase the monsters from beneath her bed.

Beneath her bed.

She added that to her list of places to double-check before she settled in for the night.

With a fatalistic sigh, she panned the interior of her SUV for anything she could use as a weapon. All she could come up with was a hard plastic ice scraper. Kayla grabbed it, pushed her car door open and got out. Feeling extremely silly carrying an ice scraper out in front of her, Kayla made her way to the front door.

She tested the knob. Locked, just as she'd left it.

She fitted the key into the lock and opened the door, switching the lights on before she stepped inside.

A quick, sweeping glance at the kitchen and living area accomplished, she entered and shut the door behind her, clicking the lock in place.

Kayla swapped the ice scraper for a kitchen butcher knife and continued her inspection, moving from one room to the next. Inside the bedroom, all was as it had been— the bed neatly made, curtains open to the waning light, her toiletries lined up on the dresser. She peeked under the bed. Nothing but dust bunnies.

A similar search of the guest bedroom and bathrooms and a final check on all the window and door locks and Kayla let out the breath she'd been holding. All clear.

She dropped the butcher knife in the kitchen drawer and headed to the bathroom, where she twisted the faucet knobs, plugged the drain and filled the bathtub. A long soak in scented water ought to soothe her fractured nerves.

While the tub filled, Kayla made a final pass through the cottage, closing all the blinds. As she passed by the huge picture window, she shuddered. Locking all the doors wouldn't stop someone from throwing a brick through the window. But there was nothing she could do there other than close the blinds and hope for the best. At least this time, she wasn't seeing shadows shifting in the dusk.

Kayla strode into her bedroom, stripping off her clothes. She adjusted the playlist on her MP3 player to something soothing and turned up the volume. She lit the few candles she'd brought from Seattle and placed them along the rim of the old-fashioned clawfoot bathtub. After dimming the lights and draping a towel over a vanity chair close by, she climbed in, sinking into the tub an inch at a time. Following the initial shock of the heated water, her body adjusted and she closed her eyes, letting the rising steam cleanse her pores and melt her fears away.

What a day. From almost falling off a cliff to the frightening news of a murder, she could use a little less excitement in her life. Most frightening of all was the necklace left in her SUV for her to find. Her attacker was here in Cape Churn—there was no denying it now. The question was, what was she going to do about it?

She could try to run. Again. But that was the problem, wasn't it? She'd left Seattle as secretly as she could to escape her attacker, and he'd still managed to track her down. Would running once more do any good?

If she stayed, what could she do to protect herself and her baby? "I guess we could move closer to town," she said, tracing designs in the trails of water over her belly, "but that might just make things worse. Out here, there's hardly anyone around—I don't have to look twice at every man who passes to see if he's the right height, the right build to be the attacker. But am I putting you in danger by keeping you all the way out here where there's no one around to help us?"

That wasn't true either, though, was it? There was someone around to help—someone who would be coming around for just that purpose very soon.

Gabe McGregor. Tall, broad-shouldered and with eyes that could light the sky, the small-town cop had been the rock in the quicksand of the day's events. The compassion in his gaze and the way he made her feel safe went a long way toward restoring her faith in humanity. It was such a relief to be around a strong, powerfully built man and feel protected instead of scared. She felt no urge to back away from Gabe. Instead, shockingly, she wanted to step closer. But she wasn't ready for that yet…was she?

With the heat, scented candles and mood-fixing music surrounding her, Kayla relaxed against the porcelain.

A noise from the other room startled her and she jerked to a sitting position. She reached for her MP3 player, turning the music off. Silence filled the room, the only sound her breathing and the thunder of her pulse against her eardrums.

"I'm hearing things," Kayla said, and sank back into the warmth of the bathwater.

A scratchy, tapping sound brought her out of the tub and onto the bare floor. Her wet feet slipped on the smooth tile and she grabbed for the sink to steady herself. She glanced at the mirror, the steam from the bath having fogged her reflection. Bold letters glared at her, clinging to the glass where the mist dripped free.

SCARED?

Kayla screamed and backed away, not realizing she was stepping in a puddle until her legs shot out from under her and she fell against the tile, her head hitting the edge of the sink. Shards of light crashed through her skull as she landed on her back, the air forced from her lungs.

Fog moved into her vision, the Devil's Shroud shutting out the light from the bulb overhead.

Kayla fought to surface from the encroaching darkness and lost. She tried to scream but no sound passed her lips.

As she faded into the abyss, pounding rattled inside her splitting head. Pounding like the waves on the rocky shore, pounding like hammers on hardwood, like feet on pavement...running, chasing her....

As Gabe climbed out of his truck, a scream ripped through the night.

"Kayla!"

He raced for the door to the cottage, grabbed it and twisted.

Locked. Lights glowed throughout what he could see of the living and dining area. Kayla was nowhere in sight.

He jiggled the door, abandoned it and ran to the back door on the side of the cottage that backed up to the lighthouse.

He tested the doorknob. It, too, was locked.

"Kayla!" He pounded on the door.

Nothing.

Back around to the front, he pounded on the window, the door, and no one responded.

His heart racing, adrenaline pumping through his veins, Gabe backed away, tucked his arm against his side and hit the door with his shoulder and bounced back, pain shooting through his arm.

He raised his foot and kicked the door next to the handle. Wood split, the frame weakening. Another well-landed kick and the jamb broke, the door flying open.

"Kayla!" Gabe ran through the living room into the bedroom. He noted the bed neatly made, nothing out of place. He moved on to the closed door of the bathroom and stopped.

What if she'd been in the shower and couldn't hear him knock? But she'd screamed—surely that meant she was in danger. With his breath caught in his throat, he reined in his urge to kick in another door and knocked instead. "Kayla, it's Gabe."

A moan from the other side of the wood paneling made the decision for him.

He twisted the doorknob and pushed.

The door wouldn't budge.

With more oomph, he pushed again. Something heavy blocked it from opening all the way.

In the three-inch gap, Gabe could make out a bare leg. "Kayla?" Carefully, he shoved the door steadily, sliding her body forward until he could squeeze through.

As soon as he was in the bathroom, he dropped down beside Kayla.

She lay on the floor of the steamy bathroom, blood staining the white tile, her body covered in nothing but a thin sheen of moisture.

Gabe pressed two fingers to the base of her throat and held his breath, praying for a pulse.

When the steady *thump, thump* of blood coursing through veins nudged against his fingers, he let out a sigh. "Kayla, talk to me." Gently, he ran his fingers along her arms and legs, searching for broken bones. Everything was where it was supposed to be, but she wasn't waking up.

"Come on." He reached for the towel draped over the edge of the bathtub and tucked it around her, turning to the cabinet for more towels. "Kayla, sweetheart, wake up." He had to get her warm to keep her from going into shock.

Towels in hand, he faced Kayla.

Her green eyes blinked open. "Gabe?"

"Yeah, I'm here." He laid another towel over her shoulders and used one to dab at the blood oozing from a gash buried somewhere in the hair above her ear. "Can you move?"

"No." A smile twitched at the corner of her mouth. "Yes. I just don't want to."

"Then just lie still while I call an ambulance."

Kayla shook her head and winced. "No, don't. I can move. Really." She sucked in a deep breath and pushed up on her elbows, the towels falling down below her breasts. "Oh." She lay back down, her face flaming, hands clutching the towels to her chest. "I seem to be missing my clothes. What happened?"

Gabe smiled down at her. "I was hoping you could tell me."

Her gaze panned the room. "I was taking a bath."

Gabe nodded toward the full tub. "Okay, and then what?"

Her brows furrowed. "I can't remember." She pushed to a sitting position, holding the towels to her front. "There was a noise and then…" Her gaze shot to the mirror and her face lost all color.

"Kayla? What happened next?"

"That." She raised a hand, her finger pointing at the mirror.

In the fading moisture on the glass, Gabe read the message, his heart sinking to his knees. If he'd had any doubt before that the killer was after her, he didn't now.

He gathered the woman in his arms and held her while silent sobs shook her body.

Anger surged through him, making him want to strike out, to hunt down this man who frightened women in a very sick game. Especially this sensitive beauty who would never hurt a soul.

Whatever it took, he'd find the bastard. And when he did, he'd never let him hurt Kayla—or any other woman—ever again.

Chapter 7

Kayla lay on a gurney in examination room one of the emergency room at Cape Churn Hospital. Rubber-soled shoes squeaked as nurses moved up and down the hallway. The doctor had already been by, shone his light in her eyes and pronounced her fit to leave, no concussion. Most important, the baby was okay, no bleeding, the heartbeat strong and normal for this stage of the pregnancy.

So what was taking so long?

She pushed to a sitting position and swung her legs over the side of the gurney. For a moment her head swam, but that was normal, too, for being pregnant. Her body wasn't her own anymore and she'd better remember it.

She caught a glimpse of herself in the mirror over the wash basin. Wearing the jeans and T-shirt she'd insisted on throwing on before leaving the cottage, her hair matted with blood, she imagined she was a sight. So much for her first impression on the citizens of the cape.

Gabe stuck his head inside the door, carrying two steaming cups of coffee, the rich aroma wafting her way. "Hey, there, mind if I come in?"

"Please do."

"Sorry, all they had was decaf."

"Perfect." She held out her hand for the cup, wrapping her fingers around its warmth. "Why do they keep hospitals so darned cold?"

"To keep out the riffraff." He smiled. "The doc is signing your release papers. As soon as the nurse has that and gives you the out-brief, you can leave."

Kayla sighed. "Good. The smell of antiseptic and floor cleaners makes me sick." She gave him a wan smile, unwilling to go into further explanation, not ready to reveal her little secret growing inside. She rubbed her hand across her belly. It wouldn't be long before the little bump got bigger and she wouldn't be able to hide her condition to the world.

She'd kept the secret from the media in case something went wrong during the first trimester and she lost the baby. The end of the trimester coincided with the attack in Seattle, and Kayla hadn't thought of sharing the news since. Who would she share it with?

A nurse who had introduced herself earlier as Emma Jenkins powered into room one, carrying a clipboard and a pen. "Oh, good, Gabe's here to take you home."

Gabe grinned. "Hey, Emma, how's it going? Much scuba diving lately?"

She shrugged, her sandy-brown ponytail bobbing. "Not lately. But I hope to next week. I'm off for four days straight."

"Do you know everyone?" Kayla asked Gabe.

His grin widened. "Just the full-time residents. Emma was the little scamp who dogged me whenever I went to the marina. Now she's old enough to go on her own." He rubbed his knuckles on her head.

Emma ran a hand across her hair, a wry twist to her lips. "You'll never let me live that down, will you?"

Kayla envied the easy camaraderie of people who'd known each other for a long time. This was the kind of community she'd like to belong to, to raise her baby in. Nurturing, loving and sometimes nosy. Pushing aside her longing, she asked, "If I'm being released, do I *need* someone to drive me?"

Emma planted a hand on her hip. "It's always a good idea to have someone else drive after you've been knocked unconscious. Besides, Gabe brought you, so your car is still back at the cottage. You're stuck with him, though he's a good guy to get stuck with." She glanced at the paper on her clipboard. "The doctor said he didn't see any signs of concussion, but he wants someone to keep an eye on you through the night."

"Through the night?" Kayla frowned.

"I'll be there." Gabe nodded to Emma. "Go on."

The nurse cast a glance at Kayla. "You really need someone with you. Hopefully for just the night."

"I hate to be a bother," Kayla said. Though the truth was that she was glad Gabe would stay. With a killer leaving messages on her bathroom mirror... A shiver shook her frame.

Emma continued reading from her list. "Call the doctor if you experience any of the following symptoms— weakness, numbness, decreased coordination or balance, confusion, slurred speech, nausea or vomiting." She glanced across at Kayla with a stern look. "Any bleeding, return to the emergency room immediately."

Kayla darted a glance at Gabe. She raised her hand to her head where the wound to her scalp had been cleaned and stitched. Maybe he'd think the bleeding part was due to the head injury. At least she hoped so. Having kept the news of her baby from the public for so long, she wasn't quite sure how to break it to anyone. Including the man who'd come to her rescue.

Emma handed the clipboard to Kayla. "Sign here and you're free to go."

Kayla scribbled her name on the paper.

The nurse gave her the instructions sheet and smiled. "Don't lift anything over ten pounds and take it easy for the next couple days." She nodded to Kayla. "I'll get a wheelchair."

"I don't need one," Kayla insisted.

"Sorry. Hospital policy. We wheel you to the door and you're on your own from there." Emma winked. "Really, though, you know where to find us if you need us. Our doors are open 24/7." She slipped out the door, the squeak of her shoes fading down the hallway.

"No excitement?" Kayla snorted. "I wish."

"I hope you don't mind, but I had the chief dust your house for prints while we've been here."

"I'm okay with whatever it takes to catch this guy." She scooted to the edge of the gurney and slipped off to stand on her own two feet. Her head swam and her knees trembled.

Gabe's arm slipped around her waist. "You should wait for the wheelchair."

"That'll only get me to the door. I have to be able to walk to my house."

"I can carry you."

Her skin warmed all over at the thought of Gabe carrying her, but she didn't want to get too used to having him around. She lived alone and she had to be able to get around by herself.

Gathering her strength, Kayla straightened, her legs holding steady. "I'm okay, really." She pushed away from him and stood on her own. "See?"

"Here we are." Emma cruised into the examination room, ponytail bouncing, pushing a standard-issue wheelchair. "If you'll take a seat, we'll get you out of here so that you might actually get some sleep in what's left of the night."

"Thanks, Emma," Gabe said. "You've been very helpful."

"Just don't go skating on wet tile in the near future." She shook a finger at Kayla. "Bad idea, especially for someone—"

"Gotcha," Kayla said, afraid Emma would say too much before she was ready to reveal her secret. "I'll be sure to dry off before I jump out of the tub from now on."

Emma pushed the wheelchair to the exit and waited with Kayla while Gabe retrieved his SUV.

"He doesn't know?" Emma stood beside her, her gaze on the SUV pulling out of the parking lot.

"No. Nobody knows around here."

"It's none of my business, but why?" She glanced down at Kayla, her hazel eyes open and friendly.

Kayla smiled. "I don't know. At first, I wanted to get past my first trimester without miscarriage, now…with all that's happened…I could still lose this baby. I don't want anyone to treat me any differently, either way."

"You sound like you could use a friend." Emma pushed a loose strand of straight hair behind her ear. Kayla nodded. Emma was right. Since Tony's death, she hadn't wanted to invest her emotions in anyone except her baby, afraid of the pain of loss. It was time she got over that. "Got anyone in mind?"

"I'm off the day after tomorrow. Would you like to come

have lunch with me at the marina? I'm getting my gear ready for a dive and they make a decent cup of joe."

Warmth spread through Kayla and she nodded. "I'd like that. What time?"

"Make it noon. I like to sleep in a little." Emma stepped forward as Gabe's truck pulled up next to the curb. While she opened the door to the SUV, Gabe rounded the front and reached out to help Kayla stand.

"Really, I'm quite capable," she said.

"Let him play the knight in shining armor, it makes him feel like a man," Emma teased.

Gabe frowned at her. "You're not helping my ego, little girl."

She batted a hand at his back. "I'm not a little girl."

Kayla laughed. "If you two could quit playing…"

"She started it." Gabe reached out and hugged Emma. "Good to see ya, kid."

"You, too. Stay out of trouble, I don't like seeing my friends here." Emma nodded to Kayla. "Day after tomorrow."

Kayla smiled and nodded.

The drive to the lighthouse cottage was accomplished in silence. When Gabe pulled into the driveway and parked, Kayla hurried to get out of the vehicle before Gabe could get around to help her.

Which was probably just as well. The more he touched her, the more he wanted to.

Gabe rounded the SUV and held out his hand. "Just hang on to me. It makes me feel more of a man." He winked.

Kayla hooked her arm through his and walked with him to the door of the cottage. Lights blazed from every room, the front door hung open, the splintered frame a painful reminder of what had happened.

Kayla waited while Gabe went in first.

Gabe glanced around, taking in the traces of black dust, barely noticeable. He checked all the corners and ducked in and out of the rooms and closets. When he was satisfied, he returned to the living area and Kayla. "Looks like they cleaned up after they dusted for prints. Otherwise, you'd have black powder everywhere."

"Remind me to thank the chief." Kayla plunked her purse on the kitchen counter and stood for a long moment, her gaze on everything but him. "Look, Gabe, you don't have to stay. I'm fine."

Gabe closed the distance between them. "You heard Emma. You need someone to keep an eye on you. Do you know anyone here in Cape Churn?"

Kayla shook her head. "Only the people I met today."

"Then you're stuck with me. Even if you hadn't bumped your head, I'd want to stay. I'm not taking that message lightly."

Kayla slumped against the counter, still avoiding his eyes. "Why is this happening to me? What did I do to deserve this?"

Calling himself every kind of fool, he—gently, tentatively—pulled her into his arms. When she made no effort to move away, he tightened his hold, nestling her close against him. Somehow he had to protect this woman. She wouldn't make it on her own. Not with a killer bent on torturing her. "You didn't do anything to deserve this, any more than that girl who died on the beach."

Knowing that she didn't need any more excitement for the night, yet realizing she'd want to know, he made the decision. "When I arrived here earlier tonight, I was on my way back from the police department to tell you what we found."

Kayla's head jerked up and she stared at him. "What is it?"

He hauled in another breath before launching into it. "We might have a serial killer on our hands."

Her face grew frighteningly pale.

Gabe could have kicked himself for saying anything, especially following the message on the mirror and the trip to the hospital.

"We ran Rachel Kendrick's murder stats through the ViCAP database and found some matches. Same victim description and all strangled. The only difference between our girl on the beach and the others was the amount of tormenting the killer did to the others before he murdered them."

Kayla's hand went to her throat, her body trembling in Gabe's arms. "I need to sit."

He led her to the sofa in the living room and sat, pulling her into his lap.

She didn't argue, curling against him, her cheek resting in the curve of his neck. "What torment?"

Her whisper blew warm against his neck, making him far more aware of her than he should be. "The killer planted things for the victims to find. Items that belonged to them that they kept in their locked homes."

"Like?" she prompted him. Her hand lay flat against his chest. She held her breath, waiting for his response.

"Favorite trinkets, photographs and…jewelry."

Kayla's fingers convulsed, bunching the fabric of Gabe's shirt. "It's him."

"I'm sorry, Kayla, but all the women had red hair and green eyes."

"Like Rachel and me…." Her voice ended on a sob.

"Her name was Rachel—I didn't even know. How very tragic."

Gabe held her while she cried quietly. What else could he do? They didn't need him down at the station. The FBI would be called in, the chief would be required to hand over the case to them since they were dealing with a serial killer and the crime crossed state lines. No, all he could do was be here for this woman.

When Kayla had spent her tears, she sat up and grimaced, eyes red and puffy, hair a mass of tangles, beautiful beneath it all. "I'm sorry."

"Don't be." He helped her to her feet and stood beside her, wishing he could hold her until all the bad in her life went away.

He knew without asking that Kayla wouldn't appreciate his overprotectiveness.

She glanced around the living area, her gaze straying, as if she was looking for something to hold on to. Finally, she spoke. "Since you're staying, do you mind sleeping on the couch?"

"Not at all."

"I'm going to get a shower and wash the blood out of my hair."

"Are you sure that's a good idea?"

"I don't care if it is or not." She touched a hand to her head and winced. "I can't stand feeling this dirty and matted."

"Need help?"

Kayla blushed. "I'll yell if I do." She hesitated. "Do you mind…"

"Checking out the bathroom? Not at all." First, he shoved a chair beneath the door handle of the damaged door, then he hurried through her bedroom and into the bathroom. Water still stood in a puddle on the tile. He grabbed the towel on the side of the bath and paused in front of the mirror. Without the steam to reveal the writing, he couldn't see the message. He didn't need to. The words had been etched in his subconscious. With the towel, he scrubbed the mirror, wiping away whatever the killer had used to write the message. Then he went to work sopping up the water on the floor. Before he left the bathroom, he pulled the plug on the tub full of cold water and laid out a fresh towel.

"That's above and beyond." Kayla stood in the doorway, a smile lighting the shadows in her eyes. She'd shed her clothes and wrapped a terry-cloth robe around her body.

His heart thudding, Gabe forced a causal shrug and tossed the used towel in the laundry basket. "Be careful."

He moved to exit the bathroom, willing himself to keep his hands off her, but she stopped him before he could go.

"Thank you, Officer McGregor." She stepped toward him and slid her arms around his waist, pulling him into a hug. He couldn't help but wrap his arms around her in return.

She let out a sigh and nestled closer. "It's as if you make it all go away," she murmured. "As if even after everything that's happened today, I know that I'm safe with you. How do you do that?"

Gabe smiled. "Just doing my duty."

"You do it very well." She lifted a hand to his cheek and rose onto her toes. Her lips brushed lightly across his, as soft as a butterfly's wing.

For a moment, Gabe froze in shock. "Kayla, is this… Do you…"

"I want this," she answered. "Please I—I want you to make it go away." Her lips brushed his again. "Please, Gabe. I need something to feel good today."

He'd had all good intentions of playing the part of the

good cop, there to protect and defend. But the kiss crashed through his defenses, laying him bare and aching.

With a groan, he pulled her to him. Careful not to touch her injury, his hands cupped her cheeks, drawing her face close, deepening the kiss.

Kayla melted against him, her hands lying flat against his chest.

His tongue thrust between her teeth, sliding along hers.

Kayla's fingers curled into the fabric of his shirt, pushing buttons free one at a time, all the way down to where the shirt disappeared into the waistband of his jeans.

He gripped her arms and held her away from him. "Are you sure this is what you want?" He stared into her glazed green eyes, his groin tight, every cell in his body on alert.

"I'm sure," she whispered. "But if you don't…" She pulled back.

Gabe drew her close. "Oh, God, yes."

With deft hands, she pulled his belt free of the buckle, flipped the rivet and slid the zipper down on his jeans.

Blood pounding, Gabe untied the belt around her waist, pushed the robe open and groaned. Firm breasts rose to greet him, taut nipples peaked to hardened points. The gentle curve of her waistline swelled out to perfectly rounded hips.

Kayla dragged his shirt down his arms, flinging it aside as her robe fell to the floor. "You have the advantage over me."

"I think you have that backward." He cupped the back of her head and claimed her lips once more.

Her hands slid down the back of his jeans and over his bottom.

Gabe dragged his mouth from hers. "We shouldn't. You've had a head injury. You should take it easy."

"That would rule out this." Kayla pushed the jeans down his hips, allowing his erection to spring free.

"Kayla…"

"I didn't plan for this to happen. And I know we probably shouldn't. But I can't help it. I need this too badly." Her lips pressed to his chest, finding the hard brown nipples, tonguing them while her hand circled his member. She paused, glancing up at him. "Tell me you don't want this and I'll stop. Otherwise, let me feel. Just for tonight. I need you."

"I might just regret this…but what the hell." He scooped his arms behind her legs and set her carefully in the tub. Then he shucked his jeans and climbed in with her, tugging the shower curtain in place and twisting on the water. With his back to the spray, he welcomed the cold water, chilling his desire long enough to slow him down.

Once the water heated, he wrapped his arms around Kayla and turned slowly until she stood under the nozzle, water running over her shoulders, dripping from her breasts and trailing down to the thatch of curls at the juncture of her thighs.

She reached for the bottle of shampoo.

Gabe intercepted. "Let me." Squeezing a generous amount of gel into his palm, he lathered then smoothed it into her tangled hair, careful not to touch the stitches.

Kayla stepped back, allowing the water to run across her scalp, wincing as it hit her injury.

For several minutes Gabe scrubbed her beautiful soft curls, letting the water rinse the suds clean. When her hair was free of blood and soap, he reached for the bodywash, squirting a portion into his hand.

Kayla held her hand out, palm up, and he doused it with the liquid soap.

In unison, they smeared suds over each other's bodies.

Gabe ran his hands across her shoulders and down over the swells of her breasts.

Kayla inhaled, her chest pushing into his palms, her rosy nipples tightly beaded. Her fingers laced in the hairs on his chest, following his ribs down to his waist and lower.

His shaft thickened, jutting forward into her palm. Gabe squeezed shut his eyes and gritted his teeth. "At this rate, I won't last long." He pushed her hand away. "Let me please you."

"But I want to touch you."

"You will." He sluiced water over her breasts, rinsing the suds away, then applied more soap and smoothed his hands over her hips and down between her thighs.

Kayla pressed her breasts against his chest, her calf rising up the side of his. "I want you inside me."

"Soon." Gabe's heart raced, his control stretched thin. He didn't think he could hold out much longer, wanting to be inside her more than he wanted to breathe. Yet, he continued his assault on Kayla, his fingers circling to weave through the curly mound over her sex. He parted her folds, slipping a finger inside to flick the nubbin of her desire.

She gasped, her hands digging into his arms. "Oh, God."

He strummed it again and she molded her body against his. "I'm on fire. Please…"

"Please what?" He dipped into her juices, swirled and returned to that special place that had her climbing up his body with each touch.

"Please, come inside me." She clamped her palms on either side of his face, her eyes wide, intense and so dark they rivaled an evergreen forest.

Barely able to stand himself, he lifted her, wrapping her legs around his waist, and stepped out onto a towel.

"We need to dry off," he said.

"No, I can't wait."

"I won't risk you falling again."

"Fine, but hurry." Her legs dropped to the floor and she grabbed for a towel and began squeezing the water from her hair.

Each time she winced, Gabe felt a stab of guilt.

"We shouldn't be doing this so soon after your fall."

"Don't you back out on me now." She advanced on him, wrapped the towel around him and pulled him against her, his member pressing into her belly.

"Okay, I surrender." He lifted her in his arms and carried her into the bedroom, laying her out on the bed.

"Do you have…"

"I'll be right back." He ran to the bathroom, fished in the back pocket of his jeans to unearth his wallet. God, he hoped he had a condom.

Buried beneath his credentials, credit and health insurance cards was a lone foil packet. As he returned to the bedroom, he ripped it open with his teeth and slid the rubber down over his engorged shaft.

Kayla smiled up at him, her damp hair curling darkly against the white sheets. She raised her arms, beckoning him closer.

He slid between her legs, the tip of his erection nudging against her entrance. "Just say the word and I'll stop."

Her legs wrapped around his waist and she squeezed.

He slid in, thrusting deep, her channel invitingly slick with her juices. Even with the condom, it felt so wonderful, so right. Like coming home.

Gently at first, he moved in and out of her, slowly increasing the pace until they rocked the bed, the headboard bumping into the wall.

Kayla's heels planted in the sheets and she pushed up

to meet him thrust for thrust, her hands on his hips, guiding him in and out.

Tension built and peaked, shooting Gabe over the edge, sparklers rocketing to fireworks as he climaxed. He pushed into her one last time and held steady, deep inside her warm, moist center.

Kayla's back arched from the bed, her face tense, eyes tightly shut. Then she cried out his name and fell back to the bed, a thin sheen of perspiration covering her body, making her pale skin glow.

When the waves of sensation subsided, Gabe lay down beside Kayla, rolling her over to face him, maintaining their intimate connection.

Her green eyes opened, glazed with passion and drooping with exhaustion. A smile curled her kiss-swollen lips. "Wow." Then she closed her eyes, her body going limp in his arms.

Gabe's heart skipped several beats. What had he done? Making love to a woman with a head injury was just asking for trouble.

"Kayla?"

She didn't answer.

He shook her gently. "Kayla? Talk to me."

"Mmm." She pressed her face into his chest, snuggling against him. "Again?" Her eyes fluttered open then closed. "I'm too tired."

A chuckle rose in his chest and he bent to press a kiss to her forehead. "Sleep, sweetheart. Everything's going to be all right."

Her breathing grew slower and deeper.

For a long time, Gabe lay with her in his arms, unwilling to break their connection. Afraid it was just a fluke and would never happen again. And he wanted it to happen again and again.

God, what was he doing? Just a few hours ago, he'd told himself that he couldn't get involved. Not with anyone, and especially not with Kayla. But he hadn't been able to help himself. He'd craved her too strongly to resist, so he'd let himself believe her when she said that she needed him to take it all away, to make it better for a little while. But had he actually made things worse? The danger hadn't lessened. The threat against her was still very real. Would he be able to keep his objectivity and protect her with a clear mind now that he knew how it felt to make love to her?

As he lay there wide awake, the events of the day crowded in on him. The murdered woman, the necklace, the writing on the mirror, Kayla lying on the floor unconscious, the ViCAP database.

His thoughts swirled, hammering against his consciousness. In the end, he couldn't lie still, he had to get up. He needed to call Molly and let her know what had happened and that he wouldn't be home that night.

Slipping into his jeans, he padded barefoot out to the living room. All the blinds were closed except the large picture windows overlooking Cape Churn.

Drawn to the view, he moved closer to the glass, disappointed by the starless night. Fog pressed against the coastline, obliterating the ocean view.

Something else blocked the view through the window. With the darkness outside making the glass mirror Gabe's reflection, he almost missed it. Then he saw it, red paint in bold, block letters, splashed across the window.

W-H-O-R-E-!

Chapter 8

Kayla woke the next morning with a dull headache pounding against her skull. She stretched, winced at her sore muscles and bruised body. As each pain made itself known, the memories of the day before flooded back. Everything from the day before. Including who she'd fallen asleep next to at the day's end.

She sat up straight, the sheet falling down around her waist. Heat rose up her neck and into her cheeks. Her naked body had beard burn in several places, and the musky scent of sex filled the room.

Her gaze shot to the bathroom. The door hung open, the light off.

"Gabe?"

The sound of an electric drill reached her. What was the man up to?

Hauling the sheet around her, she scooted off the bed

and stood. As soon as her feet hit the floor, her stomach roiled—one of the wonders of being pregnant.

Clamping a hand to her mouth, she dashed into the bathroom and sank to her knees in front of the toilet, hurling bile into the water.

"Kayla?" Gabe rushed in, worry filling his voice. He squatted beside her and held her shoulders, his hands warm and reassuring.

God, she didn't want him to see her this way. Not yet. Not when he didn't know.

"Are you all right?"

"No. I'm vomiting." Her stomach rose into her throat and she dry heaved, the sound disgusting to her own ears. How lovely it must be to Gabe's.

"That's one of the symptoms Emma said to watch out for." He popped to his feet. "I'm calling the doctor."

"No!" Kayla held up a hand, but couldn't talk as another round of dry heaving hit her full-on.

Gabe ignored her plea and ran into the other room.

As the heaving continued, Kayla remained glued to the porcelain, unable to stop the man from making a needless call.

When her stomach finally settled, her back hurt and the muscles along her rib cage screamed. She flushed the commode and pushed to her feet, wrapped her bathrobe around her naked body and stared into the freshly scrubbed mirror. She gave a silent thanks to Gabe for having cleaned the threatening words from the glass.

Then she got a look at her face.

"Ugh." Her hair had dried, matted and tangled beyond repair, like a throwback to the troglodytes. Her pale face resembled death warmed over and her breath reeked of bile.

She tackled her mouth first, scrubbing her teeth and

tongue with a healthy dollop of paste, careful not to venture too far back into her throat, lest she start the vomiting all over again. Somewhat refreshed, she set to work combing the tangles from her hair.

For some reason, though, her efforts seemed to make things worse, and she was about to throw her comb down in disgust when a big, warm hand closed around hers.

"Let me." Gabe looked over the top of her head, his sky-blue gaze capturing hers, intense and unyielding, then his gaze drifted lower to her midsection.

Her pulse skidded to a stop, held for a moment, then returned at a gallop. "You know." Her words weren't a question.

He set the brush on the counter and turned her in his arms. "Why didn't you say something?"

"It's not every day you blurt out 'Hey, I'm pregnant' to complete strangers." Her flippant words ended on a wobble.

Gabe shook his head. "Where's the father? Are you married? Will he be showing up any day?" With each question he seemed to get more agitated. He flung his hand in the air. "God, I'm an idiot! Seems I can't pick a woman who's willing to clue me in on the things that matter."

"I'm not married," Kayla leaned forward. "I was artificially inseminated with the sperm of a good friend."

Her confession didn't make Gabe appear any happier. "How good a friend is he?"

More tears spilled down her cheeks, her heart squeezing hard in her chest, the pain still too recent. "The best."

"Then why didn't you marry him? Why are you leading me on?"

"I didn't marry Tony because I didn't love him that way, any more than he loved me that way." A sob escaped. "But he was my best friend and he knew how badly I wanted a child and a family of my own. We were going to be our own little family, but then he died in an auto accident two days after the AI procedure. He was the only true friend I had."

Gabe stared at her, his jaw tight, fists clenched. "You should have told me before."

She nodded. "I wasn't ready to tell anyone. It was my grief and my secret."

"A pretty important one." His mouth settled into a thin line. "If I had known, I wouldn't have…"

"Wouldn't have made love to me?" She pulled free of his arms. "Is making love to a pregnant woman that awful?"

"No. It's just…"

Her hormones flared, blowing his reaction out of proportion. She knew she was being unreasonable, but was unable to stop the anger from rising and gaining control. "What? Are you afraid I'd claim the baby was yours?" Unfounded anger burned up her neck and into her cheeks. "Well, let me tell you, buster. This baby is mine. I want her more than I've wanted anything in my life. She's mine to love and I'm not letting anyone else have her. Do you hear me? She's mine, so you don't have to worry that I'll be knocking on your door anytime soon demanding child support payments."

Gabe stared at her long and hard. "That's not what I meant."

Just as quickly as it had risen, the anger subsided, leaving Kayla feeling tired and defeated. "Just go."

"Not until you let me have my say.… What I was going to say is that you should have told me. As the man making love to you, I had a right to know." He shook his head. "I don't know you that well, but after you were so open and honest about what happened in Seattle—and after what happened between us last night—I believed that I'd earned your trust. That's why it hurts that you would keep something like this from me. Why didn't you tell me?"

She pushed him aside and ran for the kitchen, her stomach knotting.

"Kayla, we're not finished with this conversation." Gabe followed, stalking her like a man on a mission.

With one hand clamped over her mouth, she rifled through the cabinets. Where had she put the crackers? She needed a damn cracker.

Gabe found the box of saltines in the cupboard beside the sink and handed it to her. "This what you're looking for?"

With a single nod, she yanked a sheath of crackers out of the box and ripped it open, scattering saltines across the counter and floor. She stuffed two in her mouth, closed her eyes and willed her insides to calm.

Another cracker to absorb the acid and she could breathe without fear of losing it. Kayla wiped the crumbs away from her lips and sucked in a deep breath, letting it out slowly, regretting her outburst. "I'm sorry." She turned away, her gaze on the floor, crackers clutched in her hand. "You're right, I should have told you I was pregnant before we…"

Hands descended on her shoulders. "Before we made love."

She leaned back, her body molding to his. The ridge beneath his jeans growing, nudging against her bottom.

A smile quirked her lips. At least he wasn't completely turned off by her condition. He clearly still wanted her. But did she want him? Physically, yes—there was no denying the way she responded to his touch. But emotionally, was she ready for more than the one night of comfort he had given her already? She couldn't regret reaching for him last night…but she didn't know where things were supposed to stand now. Did *he* regret what they had done? Was that what this argument was really about?

"Would the night have ended differently had you known?" she asked.

Kayla could feel his shoulders lift and fall in a shrug. "Maybe."

Her empty hand covered one of his on her shoulder. "That's why I didn't say anything. I wanted you with me. I wanted you to make love to me."

"And I want honesty from the people in my life." His voice was so cold and distant. Unlike the Gabe she'd gotten to know in the past twenty-four hours. "But really, this just reminds me that we barely know each other. That we jumped into things way too fast. If I'm going to be able to do my job—if I'm going to be able to keep you safe—then I need to get some distance back."

Kayla hugged her arms around her middle, fighting back the tears burning in her eyes.

Gabe stepped away from her. "I have to run home, change and get to work." He nodded toward the door. "I installed a temporary lock until we can have the dead bolt and doorjamb fixed. It's not the best solution, but it's better than nothing."

Kayla noted the skinny push-bolt lock he'd installed while she'd slept. "Thank you."

He pointed to a can of wasp spray on the counter. "I found that under the sink. Since you don't have a gun and probably wouldn't use it if you did, this will work almost as well."

"How will wasp spray help?" She stared at the can, imagining the nasty scent of bug repellent, and her stomach lurched.

"Keep it within easy reach. If someone breaks in, spray

him in the face. It has a ten-to twenty-foot spraying distance. Make it count and aim for the eyes." The thought of spraying someone in the eyes was horrifying—but she'd do whatever she had to in order to protect herself and her baby.

Gabe's brows furrowed as he stood halfway between Kayla and the door. "Will you be all right alone?"

He'd withdrawn from her. Kayla could feel it as surely as a draft of icy air from the air conditioner.

"Yes." She refused to let his rejection bring her down. The baby needed her to be happy, healthy and focused on the path ahead. She'd be fine without Gabe. She still had her baby. Her hand swept across her belly. *We don't need anyone else. We have each other.*

"I have work to keep me busy and the lesson with Dakota." Her back to Gabe, she walked toward the big picture windows, for the first time noticing the splashes of red across the glass. "What is this?"

"He was here again, last night." Gabe's voice was flat and tight.

Kayla's pulse hammered against her eardrums and roaring blasted in her ears as she read the word. "Whore? That sick bastard called me a whore?" She marched to the window and banged her fist against the glass. "Damn him! Damn him to hell!"

Gabe crossed the room and gathered Kayla in his arms, turning her away from the harsh red paint and the message splashed across the glass. "It's just paint. I'll bring some turpentine out and scrape it off after work this afternoon."

"Don't bother," she said, her voice harsh. "I have turpentine. I can get it off."

"No. It'll take a lot of the stuff and you don't need to be sniffing the fumes. It's not good for the baby."

She wanted to argue the point, wanted to take care of

herself without his or anyone else's help. But Gabe was right. She shouldn't be sniffing fumes of any kind, not with a baby growing inside her. "Okay, I'll let you do it. But if I wasn't pregnant, I'd do it myself."

He smiled, but it faded into awkwardness as, suddenly aware of their position, he let her go and stepped back. "I believe you. Get some rest, and if you feel any of those symptoms Emma mentioned, call me immediately."

Kayla nodded up at him, warmed by his words and the worried frown on his brow. "I'll call the hospital. You don't have to babysit me, you know."

"Someone does."

"I'm a grown woman, I can take care of myself."

Although his mouth was still tight, his face etched in stone, he brushed a thumb across her cheek. "Not with a killer on the loose," he said, his tone soft, compelling.

Gabe left and Kayla set about sweeping crackers from the floor and setting the cottage to rights. Every time she passed the picture windows, her stomach knotted and she had to fight to keep from throwing something at the red spray paint.

It was just paint. She hoped words were the worst the killer would get away with. Deep inside, she suspected things would get a lot worse before they got better.

"How many strangers do we have in town? I've already questioned twenty." Gabe paced Chief Taggert's office, back and forth, spinning around in tight, agitated movements.

"I don't know, some are getting a jump on the approaching summer season." The chief pinched the bridge of his nose, squeezing his eyes shut. "Stop pacing, you're making my head hurt."

"We can't let this psycho hurt Kayla—Ms. Davies."

He stopped and faced the chief. "He's already killed three women, including Rachel Kendricks. I won't let him kill another."

"We're not letting him kill anyone. But we have to have evidence we can take to the bank, or to the crime lab. Got any of that?"

Gabe drew in a deep breath and let it out. "No, damn ."

"We didn't even find the spray can the jerk used on the cottage."

"Did you check at the hardware store for any red spray paint purchases in the last week?"

"Did it. Nada." The chief pushed to his feet. "We've got nothing but a growing list of victims."

"No. I won't let it grow. The list stops here." Gabe slammed his fist on Chief Taggert's desk, rattling the picture of his wife that leaned precariously against his in-box. The picture teetered and toppled over, landing with a clatter on the scuffed wood.

The chief set the picture straight, his chest swelling with deep indrawn breath. "McGregor, if you can't keep impartial with the Davies woman, I'll pull your butt off this case so fast your head will spin." The older man rounded his desk and stood toe to toe with Gabe. "Your emotions are going to make you lose it, and you can't afford to lose focus. Not now. I need you and the rest of the force to be vigilant. That man is among us as we speak. None of the women in town are safe as long as he's running around free."

Gabe's fists clenched and he fought to check his anger. "It's just so frustrating. Where do we look next? He's either wearing gloves or wipes away his prints. How do we catch someone who is taking the time to cover his tracks?"

"His painting on the windows last night was sloppy. He

risked a lot, you being there. I believe our killer is as frus-
trated he hasn't gotten Ms. Davies yet as we are that we
haven't caught him. His anger is going to cost him." The
chief laid his hand on Gabe's arm. "Don't let yours cost
you. And don't lose focus."

"I know, I know. Had I been paying attention last night
I might have caught a glimpse of him." He couldn't count
the number of times he'd wanted to kick himself for his
failure to think, his complete lapse in judgment. If he had
been thinking with his head and not with what was in his
pants, he might have ended the killing spree. "I'm on it
now."

"I want you to talk to Frank Mortimer."

"The recluse up on Devil's Peak?" Gabe nodded. "On
my to-do list for the day."

"Yeah, I'm pretty sure he slid in a couple days before
our victim was murdered." The chief grabbed a stained
coffee mug from his desk, strode out into the bay of cu-
bicles to the communal coffeepot and filled his cup with
thick dark brew. He tipped the cup and sipped the steaming brew. "Ask him if he saw or heard anything last night
or the night before."

"Will do."

"And be careful of the dog. I believe he's half wolf."

"Great. Just what I need to complete my day. A trip to
the hospital for dog bite."

"I'm not saying the dog will attack, I just want you to
be prepared if he does." The chief's mouth twisted. "And
a simple dog bite would be the least of your worries if he
decides to attack."

"Any way to call Mortimer to give him a heads-up so
he knows not to set the dog on me?"

"No. The man refuses to install a phone. He's a writer
or something and likes his seclusion. And if he knew you

vere coming, he'd probably put the dog out just so it could
get to you faster." Chief Taggert returned to his office
without looking back. "I'll be on the phone with the FBI.
I hope they'll give us an agent before the day's over."

"You and me both," Gabe muttered as he walked out the
door. He climbed into his patrol vehicle and headed out of
town.

The coastline curved around the cape, the lighthouse
clinging to the land jutting out the farthest. Mortimer's
place balanced on the next point past the lighthouse.

Gabe slowed as he passed the driveway leading down
to Kayla's cottage. The whitewashed clapboard house with
the pale blue shutters gleamed cheerfully, seemingly un-
concerned with the storm brewing off the coast.

Dark clouds hovered near the horizon, thunderheads
rising high into the sky, their mushrooming tops glazed
white by the sun.

Kayla's SUV stood in front of the house, but she wasn't
outside with her paints taking advantage of the impressive
skyline or the amazing colors presented in the impending
storm. It wasn't yet noon. Hopefully, Dakota would be
coming out before too long.

Gabe preferred she had someone with her, rather than
stay out at the cottage alone. Dakota had promised to stop
by for a painting lesson after he went to the general store.

Gabe checked his watch. His son should be heading to
town soon. His gaze moved to the road in front of him and
he spotted a lone figure pedaling a bicycle toward him.

Gabe stopped on the shoulder and rolled his window
down, waving at his son.

Dakota slowed, crossed the road and dropped to the
ground beside Gabe's window. "Yeah?"

The attitude never stopped with Dakota. Gabe ignored
his insolence, more concerned about his well-being and

that of the artist alone in her cottage. "Ms. Davies had a rough night."

"I heard from Aunt Molly." He glanced toward the cottage. "Want me to skip the lesson?"

Gabe's heart warmed at his son's selfless offer. "No. I think she needs the company. I just wanted to let you know to keep an eye out. If anyone comes to the cottage, call me."

"I don't have a cell phone."

"Borrow Ms. Davies's phone."

"It doesn't always work out here. Reception sucks."

Biting hard on his lip, Gabe resisted yelling at the teen's constant negatives. "Just try, will you? Anyone."

"That could be a lot of people."

"Okay, anyone, including the police. Just call." He pressed the automatic window to roll it up and stopped. "Oh, Dakota?"

The boy had mounted his bicycle, his body leaning forward, ready to push off. "What?"

"Be careful."

The kid scowled. "I'm not the target."

"Yeah, but sometimes killers don't care about the collateral damage."

The boy stared at Gabe for a moment longer.

Gabe braced himself for more argument.

Dakota nodded. "I'll be careful." The words weren't laced with their usual sarcasm or anger, and the teen's face actually looked serious.

Gabe rolled the window up, shaking his head, feeling more positive than he had in days. There just might be hope for their father-son relationship yet.

As he turned in to Frank Mortimer's driveway and pulled up next to his house, his optimism faded fast.

A huge dog resembling a timber wolf flew off the front

porch and launched himself at Gabe's car door, hitting it with the force of a freight train.

Instinctively Gabe jerked back in his seat, even though the dog couldn't break through the metal. Although, the beast could possibly break the glass.

The animal snarled and growled with vicious ferocity, leaping over and over at the window. After a few minutes, Gabe got tired of the barrage. No one came out of the house to curtail the dog's attack and the wolf didn't seem inclined to cease and desist.

Gabe leaned on the horn, long and hard. After several seconds, he let up and stared through the windshield at the front door to the rock-and-cedar cabin. Nothing moved but the dog at his side.

He leaned on the horn again.

Finally the door banged open and a man wearing jeans, a plaid shirt and work boots, and toting a shotgun, stepped out on the porch. "Heel, Loki!" he shouted over the top of the dog's barking and growls.

Immediately the dog bounded back to the porch and leaped up the steps. He lowered to his haunches beside the man, whose grizzled countenance was all but covered in dark, unruly hair that looked as if it hadn't been cut this century.

"What do you want?" he shouted, his voice gravelly, surly.

Gabe rolled his window down enough to shout, "Could you kennel your dog?"

"He ain't gonna hurt you."

Gabe wasn't so sure. With the reluctance of a cop who'd been attacked by more than one dog in the past, he climbed out of his vehicle and stood beside it, inspecting the damage to the paint.

"Are you Frank Mortimer?" Gabe called out.

"If I wasn't, I'd be squatting on his property. Of course I'm Frank Mortimer. What's it to you?"

"Do you walk your dog along the cliff between your place and the lighthouse?"

Mortimer balanced the shotgun in his hands, his stance widening. "You got a point to your questions?"

"Mr. Mortimer, I'm Gabe McGregor, of the Cape Churn Police Department. I'm not sure if you're aware, but a young woman was murdered near here the night before last. If, while you were on your walk, you saw anything, anyone, near the cliffs beside the lighthouse, that information might help us to catch the killer."

"I ain't seen nothin'." He turned to go back inside, laying a hand on the dog's head. "Stay."

The wolf-dog remained seated on the porch, his eyes trained on Gabe, lips pulled back in a menacing snarl.

"Mr. Mortimer. If you think of anything, please let someone know at the police station. Anything, no matter how inconsequential you might think it is, could be of use in the case."

The man didn't respond, entering his house through the screen door, letting it slap in place behind him.

Gabe had no intention of waiting around. Without his owner standing in view, controlling him with words, the wolf might decide Gabe was still a threat and attack.

Slowly, Gabe opened the door to his SUV, never losing eye contact with the animal. He counted to three and slid beneath the steering wheel, slamming the door, fully expecting any move to trigger Loki.

The wolf remained seated on the porch, the snarl still lifting his lip, exposing a wicked set of canines.

Gabe let out the breath he'd been holding and shifted into Reverse. He couldn't get out of there fast enough, promising himself he'd run a background check on one Mr.

Frank Mortimer. The man had to have attacked someone. He had the temperament. Hell, the wolf could be considered a weapon.

Before he could shift into Drive, a flash of silver flew in front of him and leaped up onto the hood. Loki leaned into the windshield, growling threateningly.

"What the hell?" Gabe shot a glance to the door of the cabin.

Frank Mortimer whistled and Loki returned to his side, leaving two really long scratches in the paint on the hood and one man with a heart attack behind the wheel. He flung the door open and leaned out. "What the hell was that all about?"

Loki growled, low and mean.

"You said if I remembered anything to let you know. Well, I remembered something."

Gathering his wits about him, Gabe grabbed a pad and pen and got out of the vehicle, his heart still racing, adrenaline pumping so fast, he believed he could outrun the wolf this time.

Gripping the pen tighter than normal, he raised it to the paper. "What do you remember, sir?"

"Night before last, Loki and I were walking along the edge of the cliff as usual. He started barking at something moving out by the lighthouse. You see, Loki's got wolf hearing, can hear things I can't. Anyway, he started barking and took off. I followed, but couldn't keep up, having to move slower on account of the fog moving in and all."

"About what time was that?"

"I don't know. Somewhere around nine-thirty or ten, maybe later, I don't check my watch every time I take the dog for a walk." He frowned impatiently. "Let me finish."

"Yes, sir." Gabe scribbled madly on the pad, trying to document everything the man had to say.

"When I got to the place where the path is closest to the road, I heard a vehicle take off. I remember thinking it was kinda strange as foggy as it was getting. Should have been able to see headlights or taillights from where I was." He shook his head. "Nothing, but the sound of an engine and tires spewing gravel. Loki came running back about that time, carrying this." Mortimer held out his hand. "Didn't think much of it then, but seein' as how some girl is dead…"

A black ski mask dangled from the man's hand.

Gabe's blood ran cold. Kayla had mentioned her attacker had worn a ski mask. Gabe's imagination winged past Kayla's attack to what Rachel Kendrick must have seen and felt that night. She probably put up a good fight to rip the mask from his head.

His heartbeat speeding, Gabe reached in his back pocket for his every-ready paper evidence bag and held it out. Maybe this was the break they needed. If they could find any DNA evidence on the mask…

"If you could drop the ski mask in the bag, I'd appreciate it. I might need you to come to the station to make a statement about what you heard and saw." He closed the bag around the mask and tucked the pad and pen in his pocket. "Thank you, Mr. Mortimer."

"Yeah, well, I got a daughter, too." He turned and entered the house, held the door open and the wolf entered as well.

Gabe climbed into the SUV and drove straight back to the station. The sooner they got the evidence to the crime lab, the sooner they'd get some answers.

Chapter 9

Kayla waited to open the door for Dakota until he'd dropped his bicycle in the grass and climbed the porch steps. The more "messages" she got from the killer, the less she liked unlocking the doors. Soon she'd be so paranoid she'd be barricading herself in her bedroom, too afraid to come out.

She slapped a smile on her face and waved Dakota in, praying that she didn't embarrass herself by blushing in the company of Gabe's son. Having slept with Dakota's father left Kayla feeling awkward around the teen. How would he react if he knew?

Dakota went straight to the two easels standing in the middle of the room, his shoulders slumped, tennis shoes scuffing the floor. "I heard you fell last night. If you don't want to do this today, I'll understand." He turned toward her, his blue eyes the same color as his father's. Behind his quiet question, an edge of hope shone through.

Kayla knew it cost the teen to offer and she wanted to hug him. With a great deal of effort, she resisted, knowing that would only make him uncomfortable. "No. I want to do this. I'm thinking that by giving you lessons, I'll get back in the mood to paint."

"How do you get out of the mood to paint?" He touched his finger to a dab of burnt umber.

With a shrug, Kayla crossed the room. "Events you have no control over, for one."

"Is that why you want to teach me? So you can have control of something?"

She grinned and joined him at the easel. "You know, you're smart for a teenager."

Dakota snorted. "Tell that to my mom and Gabe, they aren't so sure."

Reluctant to get into the sore spots with the boy, Kayla chose to jump right in. "That's your canvas and palette. We're going to paint a seascape today."

The teen raised his hands. "Whoa. I don't know nothin' about painting seascapes or anything. I thought this was going to be a lesson on how to do that."

Kayla grinned, undaunted by the teen's reluctance. "That's exactly what we're going to do. You'll learn by doing. First you need to acquaint yourself with your subject." She nodded toward the picture window, cringing at the angry red paint. "There's a wonderful storm building in the distance, we need to capture it on the canvas."

"Holy crap! Who did that?" Dakota pushed past the easel and strode to the window, reaching out to touch the glass. "I hope they don't accuse me. I get off probation soon."

"No one is going to accuse you," Kayla said softly.

Dakota's head moved back and forth. "You really are a target, aren't you?" He looked over his shoulder, his blue eyes shadowed, a frown pulling his blond brows together. "How can you stand it?"

"By giving you lessons. Now, are we going to paint on the canvas or stand around talking?"

Dakota stared at her for a long time, his frown deepening. Then he nodded. "We paint." He strode across the room and lifted the palette and paintbrush she'd provided for him, balancing them clumsily. "What do I do first?"

A couple hours later, they each had a roughed-in seascape painted across their canvases, Dakota's looking remarkably like Kayla's.

The teen stepped back, his eyes wide, a smile splitting his face. "Wow, that ain't bad."

Kayla crossed her arms over her chest, putting on her best impression of an art critic, and nodded. "Not bad at all. I believe you have some natural talent beneath the long hair and baggy jeans." She set her palette on the counter and stood back. "Want to take it home?"

Dakota's smile slipped from his face. "Nah. Not yet. Doesn't it have to dry or something?"

Kayla nodded. "Or something. It does need to sit for a day or two and it could use a bit more touch-up." The light in the cottage had faded, the storm they'd been painting edged closer to the mainland, billowing clouds pushing rain their way.

"I'd better get home before it starts raining." Dakota carefully set the palette on the counter, dropping the brush into a jar of thinner and headed for the door. He stopped halfway there and turned. "Unless you want me to stay with you a little longer."

"No. I'll be fine." Kayla smiled and walked with him to the door, flipping the locks and opening it to the outside. "Are you sure you'll make it home before the rain? I don't know..." She glanced at the sky as the clouds appeared to descend on Cape Churn.

"I'll make it." Dakota stepped off the porch. "Thanks for the lesson."

"No problem." She smiled at him and waved. "You really do have an eye for color."

He grinned at her, the transformation making her catch her breath.

Before she could react, he raced back up the stairs and hugged her, then ran for his bicycle.

As he slung his leg over the seat, the clouds opened, dumping their contents.

Kayla yelled, "Dakota, come back inside. I'll take you home."

"No, I'll be okay."

Kayla took one step down toward him and immediately the rain saturated her clothing. A quick step backward put her under the protection of the eaves. "Please. I'd feel better knowing you were okay."

Dakota stood in the rain, his shirt drenched, water dripping down his face so fast he couldn't possibly see to ride.

"Please." Kayla held her breath, afraid the boy's pigheadedness would be the death of him.

At last he dropped his bike and ran back up the steps, shaking the moisture from his hair like a shaggy dog.

Kayla laughed and backed away. "I'll get my keys and an umbrella. You can pick up your bicycle tomorrow."

"I'll wait here." Dakota squeezed the water out of the hem of his T-shirt and shook his hands and arms.

Moving carefully across the tile floors, Kayla gathered her purse, keys, an umbrella and towels before joining Dakota on the porch.

She popped the umbrella open and held it over their

heads as they made a dash for her SUV. Once inside, they dried off with the towels.

Kayla glanced both ways before pulling out of the driveway and onto the highway. The heavy rain pounding in from the ocean made it hard to see and even more difficult to drive. Several times on the way toward the B and B, her wheels hydroplaned, slipping almost uncontrollably across water and asphalt. As they neared a particularly dangerous curve with a steep drop-off on one side, Kayla slowed, staying in her lane, careful not to go too fast on the dangerously wet stretch of highway.

A hard bump from behind sent her shooting forward, headed straight for the guardrail.

"Look out!" Dakota threw his arms up to shield his face.

Kayla's mouth opened to scream, but the sound caught in her throat. She couldn't waste energy on screaming—she had to concentrate on keeping control of the car so that neither Dakota nor the baby would get hurt. The right-front bumper of her SUV rammed into the guardrail and skidded along the edge, scraping the passenger side as she wrestled the steering wheel all the way around the curve.

When she could bring the vehicle to a halt, she glanced into the rearview mirror, bracing for another bump. Nothing.

Whoever had bumped into them had disappeared, leaving behind a frightened teen and an equally frightened pregnant woman.

Dakota spun in his seat, his eyes wide. "What the hell just happened?"

"We were rear-ended." Kayla eased her foot to the accelerator and said in a voice as calm as she could make it, "Please watch behind us and let me know if anyone is coming."

Dakota tugged at his seatbelt and turned halfway around. "That dude could have killed us."

Kayla nodded, her hands shaking on the steering wheel. She hurried as much as she dared to reach the B and B without risking spinning out on the standing water. When she pulled in to the parking area in front of the building, she shifted into Park and sat there.

Dakota grabbed for the door handle and yanked it open. Rain whipped in sideways. With one foot on the ground, he looked back at Kayla. "You okay?"

She nodded, afraid to speak.

"You should come in and wait until Gabe gets home. You gotta tell him about what that guy did."

"Thanks, but I have to go." As much as she was shaking, she couldn't wait around for Gabe. What would she say? How should she act after what they'd done? Besides, what kind of report could she make? She hadn't gotten a license-plate number—she hadn't even seen the other car, much less the driver.

Dakota leaned into the car, a frown drawing a deep line in his forehead. "Are you sure?" When he looked like that, he was the image of his father.

After last night's mattress gymnastics with the local cop and today's scare, she was feeling a bit too fragile to handle a meeting with the sexy Gabe McGregor. "I'm sure."

"At least let someone follow you home. What if that guy is waiting for you and hits you again?"

"I'll be watching this time." She forced a smile. "Don't worry."

He thought about it and shrugged, getting wetter the longer he stood there. "Do you want me to come for another lesson tomorrow morning?"

"I'm meeting with Emma Jenkins down at the marina

around noon, otherwise we would. Let's make it after lunch."

"Emma's cool. She's teaching me to scuba dive." He stepped away from the door, but didn't close it.

"I'll see you then," Kayla prompted, waiting for him to shut the door and walk away.

"Gabe will be home any time. I'm sure he's gonna be mad if I let you drive back to your place by yourself." Ah, so that's why he was standing there—he was stalling her until his dad got home.

"I'm an adult. I can take care of myself."

"Doesn't stop others from worrying about you." His eyes widened. "God, I'm sounding more and more like him."

Kayla smiled, her bottom lip trembling. "That's not a bad way to sound. Thanks, Dakota. I'll be fine. I need to go to town anyway and get a few things."

He looked reluctant, but nodded his agreement. "Tomorrow, then."

"Remember to come in the afternoon," Kayla called out.

"Gotcha." The teen closed the door and loped to the wide front porch of the B and B. He stood under the eaves until Kayla drove away.

"Nice kid," Kayla said to her baby, and same as always, having someone to talk to made her feel less alone. "Maybe I'll get him to help me paint your nursery. Would you like that?" But despite her attempts to lighten her thoughts, she still felt uneasy about heading home. Instead of turning toward her cottage, she headed into town, feeling the need for a bit more company than her baby could provide, and too stubborn to admit to her fear of returning to the lighthouse by herself.

The small town of Cape Churn nestled in the side of the

hills, facing the cape for which it was named. The downtown area sported several churches painted white with tall steeples, a few mom-and-pop restaurants and gas stations and the marina at the lowest point in town. During nice weather, it was probably bustling and cheerful, but today, the sailboats, small yachts and fishing boats that littered the miniature harbor were all still. No one was out walking on the decks, streets or sidewalks while the rain continued to pour.

Kayla parked in front of the Seaside Café, realizing the little bit of popcorn she and Dakota had snacked on midafternoon had been a less than adequate meal for a pregnant woman.

"Mommy's trying to be healthy, Baby, but you've got to know that I get absentminded when I'm painting. I'm trusting you to remind me when we need to eat." Her stomach rumbled as she caught a whiff of cooking food and she smiled in approval as she patted her tummy. "Good job."

She waited in her SUV until the rain lightened, then made a dash for the door.

"Welcome to the café!" A short gray-haired woman scrubbed a table with a damp cloth, then set the condiments tray back in the middle. "Can I help you?" The lady's smile, more than her words, made Kayla feel welcome. Her cornflower-blue eyes sparkled as if laughter was second nature.

"I missed lunch."

"Oh, honey, we're still serving lunch. Sit yourself down right here and let me get you a menu."

"Nora, order up!" a voice called through the window between the dining room and the kitchen. Another woman about the same age as the one she'd called Nora plunked down two heaping plates of chicken-fried steak and mashed potatoes smothered in a rich, creamy gravy on the counter.

Kayla's belly rumbled. "That smells good."

"Tastes good, so they tell us." Nora waved to the tables and the stool-lined counters. "Do you have a preference for where you want to sit?"

"The bar will be fine."

The older woman stepped behind the counter, grabbed the two plates and swung back toward Kayla. "There's a menu, have a look and I'll be back in a jiffy."

"Thanks." Kayla studied the laminated menu, the delicious aroma of home-cooked food tempting her even more as it drifted through the window of the kitchen.

"Now, what can I get you?" Nora stood in front of her, a pen poised over a small notepad.

"Though the chicken-fried steak looked wonderful, I'd like to try the broiled sea bass with the rice pilaf."

"One of my husband's favorites now that he's on a diet. Not that you need to be on a diet, honey. You could probably use a little fattening up. Your eyes are all sunken in." She frowned. "Wait, aren't you the artist lady living in the lighthouse cottage?"

Kayla's head spun with the woman's quick changes in the conversational direction. "Yes, ma'am." She held out her hand. "Kayla Davies."

The woman smiled and took her hand. "Nora Taggert. I own this dump." Her eyes twinkled. "May not look like much, but we get good reviews from both the Portland and Seattle food critics."

Kayla's brows rose. "I'm impressed." Then she frowned. "Taggert. I've heard that name."

"You met my husband yesterday morning. He's the police chief." The woman's chest swelled out. "Been the chief for nearly twenty years." Her smile faded. "And it's been almost that long since we've had anything as horrible as a murder in this town."

Kayla didn't comment, guilt gnawing at her insides. No matter what Gabe said, she was still certain that Rachel Kendrick would be alive today if Kayla hadn't come to Cape Churn. She'd always carry that sorrow with her.

Nora sighed, scribbled on the pad, ripped a sheet off and slid it into a clip on a stainless-steel carousel hanging in the kitchen window. She spun it halfway around. "Julie, got a sea bass for you."

"Coming up."

Nora faced Kayla with a smile. "You doing okay at the cottage all by yourself?"

Kayla forced a smile to her lips. Why go into the details of her terrible experiences? "I'm holding my own."

"I understand Gabe McGregor has been looking in on you." She grabbed a clean glass from beneath the counter and filled it with ice water from a pitcher. "I've known Gabe all his life." She set the glass in front of Kayla and went about scrubbing the already clean counter. "He's a good man."

"Seems to be."

"Poor guy didn't even know his son existed until several months ago. The boy's mother dumped the child on him in Seattle. Washed her hands of him like he was so much garbage." Nora clucked her tongue. "That's no way to treat someone you're supposed to love."

Kayla nodded, feeling for Dakota and for Gabe. Neither one knew about the other until a few months ago, and yet they had to coexist at least until Dakota was old enough to be on his own. Raising a teen was hard even in the best of situations. She wanted to ask about Dakota's mother, but didn't feel right about prying. She didn't need to, Nora seemed more than willing to fill in the blanks.

"That woman was one of those summer transients. Stayed in a cottage down by the water with some friends. They hired Gabe as a caretaker to keep up the yard. She was older than him by a few years. Widowed. I think her husband died in a plane wreck and left her enough insurance money she didn't have to work."

Nora drifted off to the table with the chicken-fried steaks and refilled their water glasses. When she returned, she picked up as if she'd never left. "Gabe fancied himself in love. Would have picked up and moved back to Portland with her, had she offered." The restaurant owner shrugged. "There I go talking too much."

"No." Kayla laid her hand on Nora's, heat rising in her cheeks. "I don't mind." She wanted Nora to finish the story.

"That woman left without saying a word. No forwarding address, nothing. Gabe moped around town for weeks and finally left for Seattle to join the police force. Didn't return until he got Dakota." Nora smiled. "So glad to have him back. Especially with what's happened. Can't imagine a better man out there to help my husband find this killer."

"Did you know the girl who was…murdered?" Kayla's breath lodged in her lungs.

Nora shook her head. "No. She came in that day with a group of college kids. They all stopped in here for lunch." Nora half smiled. "They were all excited about going down to the beach at night for a cookout, too impatient to drive a little farther to one that's more accessible, especially at night. I don't know what they were thinking. That trail down to the beach is treacherous even in daylight, much more so at night."

"Could she have slipped?"

"From what Tom told me, she didn't get those bruises

around her neck from a fall." Nora's voice lowered. "Someone strangled her."

For a moment, Kayla was back in that dark parking lot behind the gallery, strong hands gripping her neck, choking the life out of her.

"Ms. Davies?" Nora stopped wiping the counter and stared hard at Kayla. "Are you all right?"

The air whooshed out of her lungs and Kayla sucked in more. "I'm fine."

"You turned as white as a sheet." Nora's brow knit. "Should I call a doctor or something?"

"No, really. I'm fine." She gave Nora a wan smile. "I'm just hungry."

Nora spun toward the kitchen window, her nice face creased in a frown. She opened her mouth, but before a word escaped, a plate plunked on the stainless-steel pass-through.

"Order up!"

Nora grabbed the plate and set it in front of Kayla. "Me and my big mouth. Talking about murders and such. It's not good for the digestion. Ignore me and my ramblin's and eat up."

Kayla lifted her fork, her appetite having disappeared. For her baby's sake, she ate, every bite an explosion of flavor, making the next even better. By the time she'd cleaned her plate, her outlook and her belly felt better.

"That's more like it." Nora sighed. "You got your color back." She pressed a hand to her chest. "Don't go scaring me like that again. Next thing you know, I'll be sending care packages of food up to the cottage to make sure you're eating properly."

"No need. I just haven't gotten into a routine yet."

The door behind her opened, the bell jingling. Kayla turned on her stool.

Jillian ran in, laughing and shaking rain from her umbrella.

Lawrence Wilson followed, brushing the drops from his suit sleeves, wearing sunglasses, which Kayla found odd for a cloudy day.

"Hi, Nora. Oh, hi, Kayla. Just the person I wanted to see. Mr. Lawrence wanted to get another look at the cottage and lighthouse. He's narrowed his choices down to three, and unfortunately the lighthouse property is one of them." Her lips wrinkled. "Sorry."

"No problem. Would tomorrow be all right? I'll be away at lunchtime anyway." That would also give Gabe time to remove the paint from the window. Though Kayla knew she wasn't a whore, she didn't want the rest of Cape Churn to see the horrible word.

"That'll be great." Jillian hooked her arm through Lawrence's and herded him toward a table. "Nora, could we get a couple cups of coffee?"

"I'll be right with you." Nora laid the bill on the counter. "I'm the waitress, cashier, cook and janitor, whenever you're ready."

"Could I get a cup of decaf?" she asked, prolonging her time in the café. She was in no hurry to return to her empty cottage.

Nora poured Kayla's cup, grabbed two more mugs and the other pot of coffee and walked across to the table where Jillian and Lawrence sat.

From the corner of her eye, Kayla watched as Nora's friendly banter had the couple smiling and laughing.

How nice to know everyone in a town.

She glanced across at Jillian and Lawrence several times as she sipped more of the steaming brew. She caught Lawrence staring back at her each time while Jillian laid out printouts of the properties they'd be visiting that day.

Each time, Kayla looked away first, a twinge of uneasiness prickling her skin. Finally, she set her cup on the counter. Kayla didn't even like coffee and she'd procrastinated long enough.

Pulling a bill from her purse, she laid it on the counter with the check, waved at Nora and Jillian and left.

The rain had stopped, though the clouds were still hanging dark and full overhead. If she got lucky, she might make it home before it started up again.

Out on the highway following the curve of the cape, Kayla drove slowly, her gaze straying to the rearview mirror with each passing mile. Once, she thought she saw a vehicle behind her, but she rounded a bend in the winding coastal road before she could be sure. When the road straightened again, there it was.

Kayla's pulse leaped, but she took a deep breath and focused grimly on the road ahead. She'd seen the car this time—at least she wouldn't be caught off guard. And if she was able to speed up enough, she might be able to outpace him. Her foot jammed down on the accelerator, but the faster she drove, the faster the vehicle behind her closed in.

Her breathing grew more ragged as she fought to keep the SUV from careening off the wet road. If she could make it to the cottage first, she could get inside, lock the doors and call for help.

When she made the turn onto the drive down to the cottage, she shrieked and held on to the steering wheel until she had the SUV under control. Once the vehicle straightened, she mashed the gas pedal. She went shooting down the narrow gravel driveway, then slammed on the brakes, sliding to a stop inches from the porch.

She fumbled for the door handle, shoved it open and ran as fast as she could, keys in hand.

Another vehicle slid sideways at the head of the driveway and screamed down the gravel road toward her.

She jammed the key toward the lock, but it wouldn't go in. She was blinded by fright, deafened by the roar of blood pounding in her ears.

"Please, God. Please open." Too afraid to look back, she tried again. This time the key slid into the lock and she turned it.

A car door slammed behind her and footsteps crunched in the gravel.

Chapter 10

"Kayla! What the hell?" Gabe rushed up the front porch of the lighthouse cottage, his heart pounding.

"Gabe?" She stopped halfway through the door, her hand on the knob, and looked back.

"What the hell were you trying to do? You were driving like a maniac. Are you trying to kill yourself?" He tipped her face up to his.

The slowly fading fear in her eyes made him feel as though someone had hold of his heart and was squeezing it so tightly it couldn't beat. "Oh, baby." He took hold of her arm and guided her into the house, leading her over to the sofa. "Stay here."

He hurried back outside, closed and locked her car door, then returned to the cottage, shooting the dead bolt home behind him.

Kayla curled into the cushions of the couch, her arms wrapped around herself, but when she saw him standing in the entryway, she shook her head, straightening. "Don't look at me like that—I'm fine. It's nothing. I was just being paranoid."

"You have every reason to be paranoid. Now, tell me why you tried to race me to the cottage." He sat beside her on the sofa and slid his arm around her.

Kayla nestled against him, her cheek pressed against his uniform, her fingers curling into the fabric.

"A car hit us from behind when I took Dakota home in the rain. We almost ran off the side of the road at the drop-off."

Gabe stiffened. "Did you see the car?"

"No. It was pouring down rain—I could barely even see the lines on the street. And once we were rear-ended, it was all I could do to keep the car on the road. If not for the guardrail, Dakota and I…"

"Would be dead. No wonder you tried to race me to the cottage." He hugged her tighter. "You thought I was him."

She nodded. "Sorry. I didn't know."

"Why didn't you call the police?"

Kayla shrugged. "The car had disappeared, what could the police do? I couldn't begin to describe it, it all happened in the rain, the vehicle was nothing but a blur in my rearview mirror. Besides, I knew I'd see you soon enough."

Gabe sucked in a deep breath and slammed his fist into the armrest. "Damn the bastard!"

Kayla jumped, her eyes wide.

"I can't get my arms around this case. He's here, and I'd bet he's right under our noses, but I can't put my finger on him."

Gabe wanted to call the crime lab and tell them to hurry it up, but they couldn't perform miracles. Even if they did find a hair or skin sample on the ski mask, the killer's DNA might not be in their database.

He'd spent the day checking on more of the newcomers to the area, listing, questioning and documenting any lead he could come up with. Which didn't amount to anything. All he had was the ski mask, which may or may not have belonged to the killer and may not contain anything that would link to his DNA.

Kayla's hand rose to caress his cheek. "At least you're trying."

He turned his face into her palm and kissed the smooth, soft skin. Then he brushed his mouth across hers in a kiss as soft as the brush of a feather. "I'm still mad at you."

"I know."

He kissed her again. "Promise you won't scare me like that again?"

"I promise." Her hand tightened on his face, drawing him closer, deepening the kiss.

He let himself drink of her warmth, her softness, the gentle person she was. Then he pushed away. "I can't do this."

She blinked up at him.

"I can't lose focus." He set her on the sofa beside him and stood. "He could be watching us now."

Kayla's gaze shot to the picture window where the steely-gray, rain-washed sky had darkened into inky black.

A flash of lightning split the murky sky, followed closely by the rumble of thunder. Gabe noticed the way Kayla shivered—but she shook it off a second later, forcing a smile to her lips.

"One good thing about my speed-demon driving," she said. "I got us here before the rain started up again."

Gabe didn't reply. What could he say? That he hated that he'd scared her? That he wanted to hunt down the man who'd planted such fear in her heart in the first place? That it was nearly unbearable to stand there and not reach out to touch her? He wanted to go to her, to take her in his arms and hold her there until all the bad disappeared. But he couldn't. Not with so much at stake. Not only Kayla, but Dakota and the baby, as well.

His hands clenched at his sides.

Another bolt of lightning flashed across the window.

"I don't think he's out there," Kayla said. "Not right now, at least. A man would have to be suicidal to skulk around the cliffs in this kind of weather."

"He's still out there, somewhere," Gabe replied, his voice tight with tension, his eyes focused on the window to keep from looking at her.

Warm fingers touched him, and Gabe stared down at Kayla's hand on his arm.

"But he's not here," she said. "Not right now. It's just us." Her hand slid up his arm to his shoulder as she stepped in closer, pressing up against him.

As if of their own volition, his arms rose, cinched Kayla's waist, pulling her close, their bodies melding, his groin tightening.

"Come on, we have better places to be than this window," she whispered in his ear.

He lifted her, settling her legs around his hips and carrying her to the bedroom. Even as he stepped over the threshold, he knew, this time, there'd be no going back. He'd never be able to maintain distance between them. Their destinies were as entwined as their bodies.

Her legs clenched around his middle and she pulled back enough to slide her lips across his. She slipped her tongue between his teeth, thrusting and parrying with him in a desperate, sensuous duel.

Her center rubbed across the ridge beneath his zipper, setting off explosions of awareness he couldn't douse. "Slow down." He pushed the hair out of her face and kissed her cheek, her forehead, the tip of her nose. Why couldn't he get enough of this woman? She'd held back telling him the truth once. Hadn't he already learned his lesson about trusting women? Was Kayla any different from Siena?

"I can't slow down. I want you." She rose up and then lowered herself, the effect adding friction to his trouser-bound erection.

He grit his teeth, fighting an internal battle he was sure to lose. "We shouldn't. You've just had a scare, you're worked up—"

"And you make me feel safe. Hold me, and make the world go away." Kayla grabbed his hands and pressed them against her breasts. "Please."

Gabe moaned. "You're making it hard on me."

Kayla smiled. "That was the idea." She unhooked her ankles from around his waist and let her feet fall to the ground.

Gabe held her hips until she steadied. Then his hands smoothed down her thighs, bunching the material of her skirt, dragging it upward until he reached the thin string of her panties. He hooked the elastic and dragged them down.

She rubbed herself against his fingers, urging him closer, her hand closing over his, guiding him to her core. Warm moisture coated his fingers, which he slid up between her folds, locating the swollen nubbin of her desire.

He flicked the sensitive flesh.

Kayla's head tipped back, her hair tumbling down below her buttocks.

Gabe's other hand rounded her backside beneath the skirt, cupping her bottom, pulling her closer, while he continued to stroke and tease her core until she clung to him, gasping and calling out his name.

"Please come inside me. Now." She held on to him,

backing him toward the bed, one hand over his, cupping her sex. When she bumped into the mattress, she sat, parted her legs and brought him to her. Kayla's fingers fumbled with his thick, leather uniform belt, jerking it from the loops.

He helped her push the button free on his trousers and slide the zipper down. He kicked off his boots and unbuttoned his shirt as her hands stroked the length of him.

Blood burned his veins like fire, pooling low and heavy in his groin.

When Kayla leaned forward and touched the tip of his member with her tongue, he almost came undone. His fingers dug into her hair, careful not to touch her stitches or to be too forceful as he pulled her to him.

She took him into her mouth, her hands circling him, drawing him deeper.

Gabe moaned and withdrew, the intensity of sensations so sharp they bordered on painful.

Her fingers dug into his buttocks, urging him in and out, deeper and deeper until he bumped against the back of her throat.

Lust surged like adrenaline, he had to have her. He slid free of her mouth, scooted her back on the bed and climbed up with her.

Still constricted by her clothes, Kayla shimmied out of her blouse.

Gabe captured one of her lace-clad breasts with his mouth and nipped at the tip, poking against the cup.

Her chest swelled upward, her hands sliding the straps down over her shoulders.

Gabe reached behind her, flipped the catch and dragged the bra downward, freeing her breasts.

They were perfect, full, lush and tipped with rosy-brown nipples, puckered and tight, ready.

He tongued the tip of one, bent and nipped, rolling the nub between his teeth.

Kayla moaned, her back arching off the mattress.

Gabe spread her knees apart with his own, then he pressed his erection to her entrance, poised to thrust.

"Damn."

"What?" Kayla clutched his bottom and eased him into her.

He resisted. "Condom. Do you have one?"

She shook her head. "It doesn't matter. I'm clean. Are you?"

"I don't have any diseases."

"And I'm already pregnant, so you don't have to worry about that." She laughed shakily and dug into his buttocks.

No longer able to resist, he slid in, surrounded by her warmth, her juices easing his entry. "God, you feel good."

"Mmm. You too." She raised her knees, her heels digging into the mattress. "Harder."

Still holding back, he eased in and out of her. "Are you sure?"

"Trust me," she said.

Trust her? He'd only trusted himself for so long, depending on his own capabilities to take charge and control every situation. But he couldn't control anything about Kayla—not the killer who was after her, or the terrifyingly wonderful way she made him feel. Logic and reason told him to step back, stay detached, keep some emotional distance, but...*trust me* echoed in Gabe's head. And he realized that he wanted to.

The very thought was frightening.

Like a switch being flipped, hot turned to cold, light to dark. Gabe froze in midthrust. "This is wrong."

"What?" Kayla stared up at him, her face flushed with

passion. "Why? We're both consenting adults. I want this. You obviously do, too."

"I can't." He pulled free and rolled onto his back, an arm thrown over his face.

Kayla lay beside him as still as death.

Gabe couldn't make love to her while he was still so unnerved by his feelings for her.

"Does this have to do with Dakota's mother?" she asked, her guess dead-on.

"No." He answered immediately and without hesitation, but he knew it was a lie. He'd had other women since Siena, but after the abrupt, heartbreaking end of his first love affair, he'd always kept a degree of distance from his lovers, never letting his feelings overwhelm him. If they wanted more, he ended the relationship. He wasn't willing to give all of his heart to anyone.

Then he'd met Kayla and knew immediately that she was different.

But could he let himself open up to her in a way he hadn't done since he was eighteen? Was he ready to love like that again, to take that kind of risk? Was it even safe to do so, considering the danger she was in? Keeping a little distance before falling head over heels would probably be smarter, in terms of protecting her from harm.

"What did that woman do to you?" Kayla's fists clenched in the sheets.

Gabe rolled out of bed and gathered his clothing. "I have to go."

She pushed her skirt down her legs and slipped her blouse over her head without replacing her bra. Her nipples showed through the white fabric, taunting him.

"I'll see if the chief can spare a uniform to stand guard on the cottage. At the least, he can send one by periodically to check on you."

The smudges beneath her eyes appeared even darker as she stared up at him. "And that makes up for the fact that you're running away?"

Gabe knew he was blowing it. "Kayla, I—"

"Don't worry about it. It's obvious that you and I weren't meant to be."

"I need time."

"And I need a man who isn't afraid to love." She slid out the other side of the bed, tucking her shirt into the waistband of the skirt. "Just go."

He hated leaving with so much left unsaid, but he didn't know what to say or how to say it, if he did. "I can send Dakota down to sleep on the couch, if it would help."

"No." She pushed the hair behind her ears, but refused to face him. "Go ahead and send over a uniform if you'd like. With someone keeping an eye on things, I can manage the rest on my own. I'll lock the doors. And like I said, no sane man would be out there in weather like this."

There was nothing left to say. Gabe grabbed his belt, shoved his feet into his boots and left, waiting until Kayla clicked the lock in place before he walked down the stairs and climbed into his SUV.

He sat for a long moment, the engine running, his hands on the shift, every fiber of his being telling him to go back, finish what they'd started and damn the consequences.

But he couldn't invest his love in this woman when there was so much at stake. The risks were just too high.

Gabe shifted into Reverse, backed up and drove away, his heart burning, his thoughts in turmoil.

When he got home, he entered the B and B, heading straight for his room, hoping to avoid conversation with anyone.

Dakota met him on the stairs, coming down. "Aren't you going to stay the night at Kayla's?"

He shook his head. "No."

"Are you kidding?" Dakota threw his hands up. "Some jerk is trying to kill her and you aren't going to be there to protect her?"

"She doesn't want me there. There are locks on her doors. I called the chief from the road, and he is sending a patrol by every hour to check on her. What more do you expect?"

"I expect you to care."

Dakota's comment hit Gabe square in the gut. He did care. He cared too much.

His son continued, "She's a nice lady. Someone who doesn't deserve to die."

"Dakota, no one deserves to die."

"Yeah? Then why aren't you there to protect her?" Dakota pushed past Gabe, ran down the remaining stairs and out into the stormy night.

"Dakota!"

"Let him go." Molly sat in a chair by the fire, a book folded over her lap. "It just upsets him that she's in danger, and he can't do anything about it. He really likes her, you know. He's been talking nonstop since he got home. Kayla this, Kayla that. You'd think she hung the moon by his account."

Gabe didn't say it, but he thought she did, too. Then why the hell didn't he let her into his heart?

"That went badly, didn't it?" Kayla said as she puttered around the cottage. "Now, don't get me wrong, Baby, he's a good man and he wants to keep us safe, but…sometimes, I just don't understand him at all. Men can be like that. All we can do is hope he wises up. Soon. And in the meantime," she continued, arranging her plate with flourish, "we dine!"

Carrying a plate piled with a fresh salad and a sliced chicken breast, she sat at the dining table, within view of the big picture window.

No matter what position she chose at the table, she could see the window in her peripheral vision. The storm, flashes of lightning and rain lashing at the glass made her imagine things that weren't there.

Her imagination had always been her gift as an artist, letting her see drama and grandeur in every play of light and shadow, adding excitement to even the most prosaic landscape painting. But now her imagination seemed more like a curse, taunting her with thoughts of sinister shapes in the darkness.

One bite at a time, she pushed food past her lips, chewing because she had to, not because she could taste anything. The food lodged in her throat with each swallow.

After several bites of chicken, she set her fork beside her plate and sighed. "This is ridiculous. I refuse to be afraid of my own shadow."

Squaring her shoulders, she lifted her fork and ate with determination to get through the meal before she retreated to her bedroom, locked the door and hid beneath the covers.

Then, a dark image passed by the glass.

Kayla's heart stopped, her hand froze halfway to her mouth and her breath caught on a silent scream.

Just as quickly as the image appeared, it vanished.

She dragged air into her lungs and let the fork clatter to her plate. Was that her imagination again? It had seemed so real. Should she call the police?

Loud thumping on her door gave her at least one answer—the figure she'd seen was definitely real. She leaped to her feet so fast, the chair crashed to the floor behind her.

"Kayla!" a familiar voice called out. "Let me in!"

"Dakota?" Kayla inched toward the door, her voice growing louder. "Dakota, is that you?"

"Yes, let me in. It's starting to hail."

Kayla let the breath she'd been holding out on a whoosh and ran for the door. She moved the chair she'd propped against the handle, pulled back the little bolt Gabe had installed that morning and flung open the door.

Dakota pushed through, blustery wind splattering the floor with rain, the porch overhangs doing nothing to keep the sideways spray from reaching inside the house. Pea-size hail pinged against the wood decking and roof.

Kayla slammed the door behind the teen and shot the bolt home. "What are you doing here?"

Dakota frowned. "I'm staying here to protect you, even if Gabe won't."

"I told him to go home."

The boy shook his head. "After what's happened, he sure as hell should have stayed." He blushed. "Sorry. Didn't mean to cuss. But you need someone looking out for you. Gabe told me about that person attacking you in Seattle. If he's followed you here, he could be the one who tried to run us off the road earlier."

Her heart swelled at the determined look on the teen's face. A tall, skinny lightweight, he wouldn't be much in the way of defense, but he was like a bulldog in his tenacity. Much like his father. "I can lock the doors. Plus, I'm sure your dad had the police chief promise to send an officer by periodically to check on me."

The boy snorted. "And what about in between checks? That douche bag could be in and out before they finish their coffee and donuts."

Kayla smiled. "They don't have a donut shop in Cape

Churn." She laid a hand on Dakota's arm. "Really, you shouldn't stay. I can take you home."

"I'd just come back and camp out on your porch." He looked at her with the stubborn countenance of his father. "Please. It would make me feel better knowing someone was with you."

Kayla chewed on her lip, admitting to herself, if not to the boy, that company helped take her mind off the shadows drifting by the windows. "Only if we can get hold of your father to let him know you're okay and that you'll be staying."

Dakota's face broke out in a grin. "Great. I'll take the couch." He flopped onto the couch and glanced up at her. "Don't mind me at all. I brought my video games." He held up his portable gaming device.

Kayla laughed, unable to resist returning the boy's smile. Given time and a chance to bulk up, he'd be just as handsome as his father. She grabbed the phone from the counter and handed it to the kid. "They turned on my landline today, so this should be working. I'm just going to take a shower. Make that call, will ya?"

Dakota nodded and punched in the number.

Not wanting to eavesdrop, Kayla headed for her bedroom, grabbed a towel from the shelf, returned to the living room and tossed it over the sofa at Dakota. "Dry off before you soak the sofa, too."

He nodded, his ear pressed to the telephone.

After a shower, Kayla slipped into her nightgown and bathrobe and stepped out of her room.

Dakota had fallen asleep on the couch, his gaming device lying on the coffee table beside him.

No, the boy wouldn't be much in the way of defense should someone try to attack her, but having him there made Kayla less jumpy and she appreciated that.

On the flipside, she also knew he couldn't stay forever. If it weren't for the terrible weather, she'd hesitate to even let him stay the night. It was one thing to have police officers checking on her—they had training, and weapons they could use to defend themselves. Dakota was just a boy. If her attacker came and Dakota got hurt trying to stop him, Kayla would never forgive herself.

She lifted the telephone to dial the number for the bed-and-breakfast. Before she finished, a loud crash made her fumble and almost drop the phone as glass shards spewed into the living room.

Kayla screamed and dropped to the floor.

"What the hell." Dakota jumped to his feet.

"Get down, Dakota!" she shouted, crawling across the floor behind the sofa and around to where he stood.

"Geez, get a load of that!" He pointed to a baseball-size hole in the picture window. Rain slashed against the gash. Lightning flashed and thunder boomed louder than before.

Kayla grabbed the teen's pant leg and tugged. "Get down in case he does it again," she hissed.

"Right." Dakota dropped to a squat and frowned at her. "You should be in the bedroom, not out here. I'll call the police." He grabbed the phone from Kayla's grip.

Moving behind the couch with Kayla, Dakota punched in 911 and held the phone to his ear. His brows veed. "Nothing. The line's dead."

Her heart hammering against her ribs, Kayla tried to think. "My purse is in the bedroom. We can try the cell phone."

"I'll get it." Dakota bunched up as if to stand.

Kayla pressed a hand to his shoulder. "Stay down. We'll go together."

"You go first." Dakota waited for Kayla to crawl several feet across the wood floor, then followed.

They'd made it as far as the kitchen when a bright bolt of lightning lit the night, followed by an immediate crash of thunder. The lights blinked and extinguished like a candle blown out.

"Keep going," Dakota urged.

As Kayla's eyes adjusted to the darkness, she moved forward haltingly, waiting for lightning to illuminate her direction.

As she neared her bedroom door, another boom of thunder rocked the house, ending in a loud banging.

Kayla ducked behind the kitchen counter, grabbed for Dakota and pulled him in close to her.

"Think it's him?" Dakota asked.

"I don't know." Kayla struggled to keep her voice calm so that she didn't scare the teen. "But we're going to be all right." She eased open the drawer above her and fished for a butcher knife, wishing she could stand and grab the can of wasp spray Gabe had left on the counter several feet away from where they hid. When her fingers closed around the handle, she lowered her hand, armed and ready. "I don't know who it is, but I've had enough."

"What are you going to do?" Dakota asked.

"Stay down."

"No. You can't take on a full-grown man."

She pushed to her feet as someone pounded on the cottage door again. "Just watch me."

Chapter 11

Gabe sped down the treacherous highway, hands clutching the steering wheel with a death grip, his tires hydroplaning in the deluge settling in puddles on the pavement.

He shouldn't have let Dakota go. With the weather as bad as it was, the boy could be struck by lightning, hit by a car or fall off the drenched roads down a nasty cliff. Guilt wadded in Gabe's gut at his son's parting comment.

Dakota had expecting him to care. Problem was, he cared too much to keep perspective and focus on the case. But the kid had it right, he never should have left Kayla alone. When he pulled in to the driveway of the cottage, there wasn't a single light on at the cottage. He jammed his foot to the accelerator, blasting down the driveway, coming to a skidding halt in the rain-drenched gravel.

He was out of the SUV and racing for the door before the engine quit turning over. Between the sheets of rain pouring down and the utter darkness of a stormy night, he could barely see to make his way to the porch. A flash of lightning lit the porch steps.

He took them two at a time and pounded on the door. No one answered, no sounds emanated from inside. "Kayla!" he shouted at the same time as another bolt struck so close, the thunder drowned his voice.

All he could think was Kayla and Dakota might be lying dead or dying on the floor. He should never have left her.

With a deep breath, Gabe reared back, cocked his leg and kicked the door where he remembered he'd installed the temporary lock. The wood jamb splintered and the door crashed inward, more easily than the first time he'd bashed in the door.

Without missing a beat, Gabe ran in.

A shadowy figure barreled toward him and a flare of lightning glinted off steel raised overhead—the sharp blade of a very large knife.

Gabe grabbed a wrist and held it high, recognizing it as that of a woman.

Before he could say anything, she kicked at his shins. "Leave me alone, damn you."

He shook the knife from her hand and it clattered to the floor. "Kayla, honey. It's me, Gabe."

The next flash of lightning illuminated her face. Her eyes widened. "Gabe?"

"Yeah, baby. It's okay."

"Gabe?" Dakota stepped up behind Kayla. "Thank God, you came back."

Gabe pulled Kayla into the curve of his arm and patted Dakota's arm. "What happened?"

Dakota filled him in, talking so fast Gabe had to stop him and have him start over twice before he got the full story.

Outside, the thunder rumbled farther away and the torrential rain that had been pounding at the roof lightened to a soft drizzle. The lights blinked, blinked again and came on.

Kayla breathed in and let it out in a rush, then pushed away from him. "Dear Lord, I almost killed you." She ran her fingers over his chest, her eyes glazed, her hand moving in jerky circles.

He grabbed her wrist and held it steady. "It's good to know you can defend yourself."

She forced a laugh though she felt no humor in the situation. "Yeah. Look how quickly you disarmed me."

"I'm trained to react and disarm quickly."

"Hopefully the killer isn't," Dakota remarked. He'd wandered across the room and was squatting next to a large stone. "This must be what he threw through the window." He started to reach for the rock.

"Don't touch it," Gabe commanded. "It may have fingerprints on it."

Dakota raised his hands in a surrendering motion. "Right. I knew that." He stood and backed away, staring from the rock to the window.

"How long ago did the rock come through the window?"

"Five minutes before you got here, maybe." Kayla stared at Gabe. "Why?"

"He might still be around." Gabe's jaw tightened. "You two stay here. In fact, lock yourselves in the bedroom. I'm going out to look around."

Kayla's eyes widened. "No."

"No," Dakota said at the same time.

Gabe gave a half smile. "I'll be okay. Chances are he's long gone."

"And if he isn't?" Dakota stepped up beside Gabe. "I'm going with you."

His chest swelling with a pride he hadn't known before,

Gabe laid his hands on Dakota's shoulders. "I need you to stay and protect Kayla in case the killer circles around."

Dakota frowned as though chewing on the options. "Okay, but hurry back. With the dead bolt busted, the bedroom door won't hold long."

Gabe liked the way the boy thought through things. "You've got that right. I won't be far. Now, go, lock the door."

"Come on." Dakota hooked Kayla's arm and started toward the bedroom door.

Kayla remained rooted to the floor, resisting Dakota's efforts to guide her into the bedroom. "Be careful."

Something different from pride filled Gabe's chest. He wanted to stay and pull Kayla back into his arms, to wipe away the worry wrinkling her brow. "I have to check outside. It's my job."

Kayla nodded, stared hard at him, then turned and let Dakota lead her into the bedroom.

On the way, the teen scooped up the butcher knife, balancing it in his hand.

When the lock clicked in place, Gabe left the cottage, pulling the broken door closed behind him. He'd have to fix that later. For now, he needed to see if their murderer was still on the prowl.

He circled the cottage, easing around the corners hoping to surprise the culprit. Between the receding flashes of lightning, he caught glimpses of the rocky terrain, but no sign of a man.

The rain had stopped and a thick mist rose, cloaking the land in a light fog that grew more dense by the minute.

When Gabe came to the side of the house with the picture window, he slowed, bending low to check for footprints. The earlier hard rain had washed away any traces of the intruder.

He straightened, glanced in the direction of the cliffs and the sea, barely visible now through the mist. If a man wanted to escape, he'd be better off going for the road. Gabe's gaze swung up toward the highway. Clumps of trees and bushes dotted the hillside between the lighthouse and highway. If he were trying to hide a vehicle, and didn't want to get stuck in the mud, the trees closest to the road made the most logical place.

As he walked toward the stand of evergreens, the fog thickened as if working with the killer to make it hard for Gabe to find him. Before long, he couldn't see any farther than four feet in front of him.

When the first tree loomed into view, Gabe jumped back, his heart racing. He chuckled quietly at his own paranoia. At the next tree, he didn't flinch, moving forward, hopefully toward the road. He'd need the road now to find his way back to the cottage. Cutting across would be far too dangerous. He might end up walking off a cliff.

A stick popped beside him and Gabe darted to the side, emerged onto the road and stumbled into the side of a dark sedan parked on the shoulder.

Something hard and thick smashed down on the back of his skull. Stabbing pain flashed like lightning through his head, sending him crashing to the soaked ground, his vision blurring.

He tried to get up, but his body wouldn't cooperate. He knew he had to stop this man before he got to Kayla.

Footsteps tromped through the gravel, moving away. A car door slammed.

Pressing his hands to the soaked ground, Gabe pushed again. He made it to his knees before a wave of pain shook his arms and he dropped to the earth.

A car engine started and tires spun onto wet pavement.

Need to see the license plate. Need to call for backup. Need to get up.

The Devil's Shroud descended, blocking Gabe's vision, sending him into a deep, dark abyss.

Kayla paced the bedroom floor, wringing her hands. "He's been gone too long. Something's wrong."

Dakota glanced from her to the door and back. "He said to stay here until he got back."

Fifteen minutes had been a long time, twenty was too much for her to take. "He's in trouble." Kayla marched for the door.

The teen stepped in front of her. "Where are you going?"

"Out to find Gabe." She tried to push the boy aside, but he stood firm.

"He wanted us to stay put. What if the killer is out there?"

"That's what I'm afraid of. He could have attacked Gabe." She looked up at the tall, gangly youth. "If he's bleeding, he could die if we wait too long to find him and get help. Let me by."

The boy hesitated. "I don't know."

"Now is not the time to follow orders, Dakota." She cupped the boy's face. "What part of your father possibly dying don't you understand?"

Dakota frowned. "Okay, but I'm in the lead."

"Whatever, just let's go." Something surged inside Kayla. Call it worry or intuition, it made her body shake with the need to take action. In her gut she knew Gabe was hurt. He wouldn't have been gone as long as he had unless something had gone wrong.

Dakota unlocked the bedroom door and led the way through the house.

"We need a flashlight. Check everywhere—find one!" Kayla rifled through the kitchen drawers to the right of the sink.

Dakota took the left side of the counter. With no luck in the kitchen, Kayla searched the front closet while Dakota took the pantry.

"Here! I found one." Dakota emerged holding up a flashlight. He flicked the button and light shone through the lens.

"Good, let's go." Kayla arrived at the splintered door first.

Dakota reached around her and held the knob. "Me first."

"Then go," she said impatiently.

He pulled open the door, glanced right then left and stepped out into the night, Kayla following close behind.

As soon as they stepped down off the porch, the intensity of the fog hit them like a brick wall.

Dakota stopped short, Kayla running into his back.

"I can't see anything." Dakota edged away from the cottage.

Kayla grabbed his shirt and tugged him back. "Not that way. The cliffs are that way."

Dakota stammered, "Y-you don't think…"

"No. I don't." Gabe was too smart to run himself off the cliff. She pointed Dakota toward the side of the cottage. "Let's look around the cottage first. Maybe he tripped over a rock."

"Or was stabbed."

"Dakota," Kayla warned.

"Just saying." Dakota leaned a hand on the side of the cottage, working his way around the corners. "Now I know what pea soup looks like. Remind me not to eat it."

"Just keep going." Worry formed a tight knot in Kayla's belly. "He has to be here somewhere."

"Or not," Dakota muttered.

She smacked his back softly. "Stop being so damn negative."

"Okay, okay. I don't like that he's not back yet either." Dakota's voice lowered. "I talk a lot when I'm nervous."

"He has to be okay." Kayla's voice shook.

When they'd conducted a full circle around the cottage, frustration drove Kayla to the breaking point. "We have to find him. He's hurt. I know he is."

"Now who's being all negative?"

The two of them came to a stop near Kayla's SUV.

Dakota walked the length of the vehicle, staring out into the murky night. "Can't see a thing. Where is he?" The flashlight beam bounced off the mist, creating a bubble of light around Dakota. When he turned back toward her, his eyes widened. "Hey, someone wrote on your back windshield."

Kayla's chest tightened. She didn't want to ask what was there.

"Geez. This guy is sick."

"W-what did he write?" she asked, her voice flat, a dull ache spreading from the base of her skull to her temples, throbbing with every heartbeat.

"They won't always be around."

A hard knot formed in Kayla's throat and she struggled to swallow past it. "Words. They're only words." Her voice shook as badly as her hands.

A scuffling sound on the gravel beyond the car brought her head up and Dakota scrambled back to stand in front of her.

"Don't come any closer, we're armed." Dakota stood

with the flashlight in one hand and the butcher knife in the other.

The scuffling moved closer and a figure materialized out of the mist. "Put down the knife. It's me."

Gabe lumbered toward them, a hand pressed to the back of his neck, his gait clumsy.

Kayla pushed past Dakota and threw herself at Gabe. "Oh, thank God!" When she hit him, he staggered backward and they both almost fell. She let go and slipped her shoulder beneath his arm. His clothing was drenched and cold. "Dakota, get his other arm, help him inside."

"I'm okay, really," Gabe protested.

"Yeah, and I don't have a killer after me. Shut up and let us get you inside."

He chuckled and winced. "Yes, ma'am."

Dakota pulled Gabe's arm over his shoulder. The boy wrapped his arm around his father's waist and took the bulk of the man's weight.

Together they maneuvered Gabe to the cottage.

Kayla released her hold and ran ahead to the bathroom for a dry towel. On her way back through the bedroom, she snatched a blanket from the bed.

Dakota lowered Gabe to a sitting position on the couch.

"Thanks," Gabe said.

"What happened?" Kayla asked, slinging the towel around Gabe's shoulders.

He raised his hand to the back of his head and ducked, wincing. "Careful. Your rock thrower hit me in the back of the head."

"Let me see." Kayla pulled his hand away from his head. His fingers were stained dark red and his hair dripped watery blood. "Dear God." She glanced at Dakota.

Dakota had lost all color in his face. If he didn't remember to breathe soon, he'd pass out.

"Dakota," Kayla said slowly. "Get a dish towel from the drawer in the kitchen and wet it thoroughly with clean water."

When the boy didn't move, Kayla spoke sharply, "Dakota, go!"

The teen jerked, his gaze lifting from the blood to Kayla's face. "What?"

"Get a wet dish cloth from the kitchen."

He ran for the kitchen. By the time he returned with the wet towel, he'd regained the color in his cheeks. "What do you want me to do now?"

"We need to get him out of his shoes. He needs to be warm and dry or shock could set in. I'll call the ambulance."

"No." Gabe pushed to his feet. "I don't want an ambulance driving off a cliff in this fog."

"Then I'll drive you to the hospital. You could have a concussion."

"I'm fine, but for a headache the size of the lighthouse."

"Lie down, then, and let me try to call the hospital. If I can reach them, they should be able to tell me what to do." Kayla rested her hand on his shoulder, urging him to lie back on the sofa.

He brushed her hand aside and peered up at his son. "Dakota, shove a chair under the doorknob."

"Yes, sir." The boy grabbed a kitchen chair and shoved it under the knob, securing the door with the broken lock.

"Thanks." With the door secure, Gabe leaned back and winced. "He got away—I heard him drive off. But he could still come back."

"Did you see him?" Dakota asked.

"No. He sneaked up behind me and hit me before I could move out of the way. The fog was so damn thick."

Kayla's chest hurt. "You shouldn't have gone out."

"And let him get away?" His lips twisted. "Oh, wait, he did get away." He grabbed Kayla's hand. "I'm sorry. I almost had him."

She patted his hand. "I'm glad you'll live. You scared the two of us half to death."

"I would have been back sooner, but when I came to, I was disoriented. I didn't know where I was or which direction to go."

"At least you didn't fall off a cliff," Dakota offered.

Gabe glanced across at his son. "Glad you feel that way."

The teen scuffed his shoe on the wood flooring, his gaze on his toe, not his father. "Hate to have to break in a foster parent," he muttered.

Kayla suppressed a grin, the tightness in her chest loosening now that Gabe sat on the couch with her and Dakota. For a while there, she'd imagined all kinds of scenarios, none of which had a happy ending. She took the wet towel from Dakota's hand and dabbed at the gash at the base of Gabe's skull. "You have a knot the size of a goose egg back here."

"I'll live."

"This time," Kayla added, her joy at finding Gabe fading as the magnitude of what might have happened sank in. "He could have killed you."

Gabe caught her wrist and pulled her to stand in front of him. "He didn't."

"He wouldn't have tried to kill you if I wasn't here at Cape Churn. Just like I told you before, this is my fault."

"What?" Dakota's eyes widened. "How can you even consider this to be your fault?"

Gabe grinned. "See? Even my son agrees. This isn't your fault. The monster who's after you is a lunatic. He's a few fries short of a combo meal and he's got his sights set on you. You did nothing to bring about his attacks."

"How do I know?" Kayla stared down at where Gabe's fingers wrapped around her wrist. "I could have been ugly to a stranger in Seattle. He could be that stranger."

"First of all, you could never be ugly to anyone and second of all, the killer is responsible for all his actions and reactions to others. He's sick, Kayla, and that is not because of you."

She nodded, knowing he was right, but feeling responsible for bringing the wrath of a killer down on the quiet seaside community of Cape Churn. "I don't want anyone else hurt."

"Neither do I."

"Then how do I make him stop?"

Gabe's hand slipped from her wrist down to her hand and he held it. "You don't." He glanced up, his eyes narrowed, intense. "I do."

Gabe meant to catch the killer.

Kayla just hoped the murderer didn't kill him first.

Chapter 12

Gabe strode into the police department offices earlier than usual, headed straight for Chief Taggert's office.

The chief shot a glance at his watch and looked up, brows rising to the thatch of thick gray hair. "You're up early. Storm keep you awake?"

"Had trouble out at the lighthouse cottage."

"The midnight shift filled me in. You feeling okay? I have Rodney on standby in case you couldn't make your shift."

"I'm fine. But things aren't great with this case."

"You're telling me?" Taggert shook his head. "The parents of the victim have been calling me every day, wanting answers. I got a special agent calling me for details and if that ain't bad enough, Jess Frantzen rang me five times this morning wanting to know what I was gonna do about his missing four-wheeler.

"Frantzen lost a quad?"

"No, someone stole it out of his locked shed last night."

"Forced entry?"

"Yup. Cut right through a padlock." Taggert shoved a hand through his unruly hair and sighed. "Only bright spot in my day is that the fog lifted about an hour ago."

"Weatherman said it'll be back tonight."

"Maybe I should bring in everyone for duty tonight. The way things have been going, that ding-danged Devil's Shroud will make this place even more chaotic than it's been already."

"Any word from the crime lab?"

"Nothing yet. I'll give them a call in an hour. It'll give them a little more time to get to work. Not everyone gets up at the butt crack of dawn like you."

Gabe smiled. "And you."

"Comes with the job. Besides, my wife's Yorkie won't let me sleep past five-thirty, even if I wanted to."

"Can't believe you put up with that little rat." Gabe shook his head. "Last time I was over, he peed on my foot."

The chief chuckled. "Truth is, the little guy likes me better than Nora. I kinda like him, too."

"Dogs have a way of getting under your skin." Gabe remembered the beagle he'd had as a child before his parents divorced and his mother moved him and Molly to Cape Churn. Then she didn't have the resources to take care of another creature. It was all she could do to make rent and utilities and keep Gabe and his sister in clothes as fast as they'd grown. He remembered Butch, though, and the memory brought a smile to his face.

Maybe that's what Kayla needed. A dog to protect her until they caught the killer.

"Did you get around to questioning all the transients in town?" Chief Taggert asked. "Any of them look like a killer?"

"I'm halfway through the list. So far, they're mostly re-tired couples, fishermen and young families. I don't know. Why don't you tell me what a killer looks like and I'll go right out and arrest him?" Gabe slouched in the only clear seat in the chief's office.

"That's a talent I have yet to acquire." The chief sighed. "If only it was that easy."

"What's the final on how the young woman died?"

"Strangulation. Our perp choked her to death."

Gabe drew in a long breath and let it out. "So young." And too much like Kayla.

"Where's the artist right now?"

Sometimes Gabe could swear the chief was a mind reader. "I followed her to the B and B. She's with my sister for part of the day."

"Probably just as well. I can't afford to keep an officer on her house at all times. I'll be glad when the FBI steps in."

"When will that be?"

"If not late this afternoon, then tomorrow morning." The chief clicked on his computer, bringing up his email. "There." He poked his finger at the screen.

Gabe leaned over the man's shoulder.

"The only agent they had available is on his way back from D.C. He's flying into Seattle tonight. Driving down when he gets there."

"About damn time." Gabe straightened. Until the agent got there, they had to keep Kayla alive. With the killer's constant taunts, it was only a matter of time before he made his move.

"I want you to check in on Andrew Stratford. I went by there yesterday and didn't get an answer. He's not taking phone calls either."

"Hasn't he been a longtime resident of Cape Churn?"

"Sort of. He comes periodically, but never stays long. He just recently got back in town."

"Is he a suspect?"

"Let's just call him a person of interest. The man is a loner, fresh back to town. Ah, hell, I don't know who to suspect, but it's better checking on him than leaving him off the list. See if he has a motive. He's had the opportunity to be in Seattle around the time Ms. Davies was attacked."

"I'll also run by the hotel in town and see if I can catch Mr. Wilson."

"Lawrence Wilson?" the chief asked. "The man Jillian's been showing property to?"

"Yes. He's only been in town for a week. Might as well question him as well. Says he's from Portland. Wouldn't hurt to run a scan on him through the DMV to check his story."

The chief made a note and looked up. "Let me know what you learn."

"Will do." Gabe left the station and headed for the rocky point on the other side of Mortimer's place.

Andrew Stratford's estate lay behind a huge wrought-iron gate. After buzzing the call button several times, Gabe gave up, got out of his cruiser and climbed over the fence, careful not to get caught on the pointed ends of the posts. He dropped to the ground and straightened his uniform.

The grounds had seen better days. Hedges were overgrown, the trees needed dead limbs trimmed and grass crept in on the sides of the paved road leading toward the Stratford mansion.

Leery of guard dogs, Gabe walked the road, one hand resting on his nightstick, the other on a pistol.

As he neared the house, a large black dog barreled around the side of the house toward him.

Gabe took up a ready stance, his nightstick held out in front of him before he realized the dog was a gangly Labrador with a wagging tail, followed by a giggling little girl with long, pale blond curls floating out behind her.

When the dog spotted him, he changed course and ran straight for Gabe, with the little girl calling out behind him, "Brewer, stop! Give me back my doll!"

The dog never slowed.

Gabe bent and braced himself for impact.

Brewer dropped the doll between his teeth and plowed into Gabe, nearly knocking him off his feet.

Several minutes later, the dog stopped jumping on Gabe and started planting slobbery kisses over whatever part of Gabe's body he could reach. When he'd tired of greeting Gabe, he made a grab for the doll on the ground.

Gabe beat him to it, holding the little girl's toy out of Brewer's reach. A squirrel ran up a nearby tree and the dog took off after it.

The child stood several feet away from Gabe, her face solemn, her gaze pinned to the doll in Gabe's hand.

"Is this yours?" Gabe asked.

She nodded.

He held out his hand, but the little girl wouldn't step closer.

"Is your daddy home?"

The little girl nodded again.

"I won't bite. I'm a police officer. I need to talk to your daddy."

She still didn't talk.

When Gabe stepped forward, the little girl stepped back, her eyes widening, her body tensing as if gearing up to run.

Gabe held up his hands. "It's okay, I won't hurt you.

Here." He laid the doll on the ground and took several big steps backward. "Go ahead."

She stared at the doll and back at Gabe, then turned and ran, leaving the doll on the ground at Gabe's feet.

"You're trespassing," a voice said behind him.

Gabe spun, facing a man probably around the same age as Gabe, mid-thirties, pitch-black hair, blue eyes. "My apologies. I couldn't think of any other way to see the owner. Are you Andrew Stratford?"

The man nodded. "Yes. Why are you here?"

Gabe had never met Andrew Stratford, the man hadn't lived at the Stratford estate when Gabe was growing up. Only old man Stratford, Andrew's grandfather, had lived there. Everyone thought the old recluse was crazy.

Gabe wondered if Andrew took after his grandfather, pitying the little girl who lived with him.

Andrew turned toward the drive leading up to the house. When he did, Gabe noticed a long, puckered scar along his jawline, reaching up to the corner of his eye.

Gabe bent to retrieve the doll on the ground. "This belongs to the little girl."

Stratford took the doll. "Thank you. Now, if you're done rescuing toys, perhaps you could leave."

"I'm Officer McGregor, with the Cape Churn police department. I need to ask you a few questions, Mr. Stratford."

"What's this about?" Stratford turned the scarred side of his face away from Gabe's view, his eyes narrowing.

"Are you aware there was a murder two nights ago near the Cape Churn lighthouse?"

"Yes. I'd heard." He crossed his arms over his chest. "What does that have to do with me?"

"We're questioning everyone who might have been near the lighthouse and seen or heard anything that night."

"I know nothing about the murder, didn't see anything either."

"Can you tell me where you were the night before last around midnight?"

Again, the man hesitated. "Am I being accused of the woman's murder? If so, I want my lawyer."

"No, sir. We're just covering all the bases." Gabe made a mental note to check Andrew Stratford's police record. "Where were you two nights ago around midnight?"

"I often walk along the cliffs at night."

"Even in the fog?"

He nodded. "It calms me. Not that it's any business of yours... That night, I didn't walk as far as the lighthouse. The fog became too dense, I turned back halfway between."

"Sir, did you see or hear anything while you were walking?"

"As I said, the fog was too dense. I didn't see much. The waves on the shore were all I heard."

Gabe put his notebook in his pocket and held out his hand to shake Stratford's. "Thank you, Mr. Stratford. I appreciate your time."

Stratford lifted his right hand, but clutched it in his left instead of extending it. It too had the puckered scars of a serious burn.

Dropping his hand, Gabe turned to see the little girl standing by the side of the house, staring at him, her hand on the dog's head.

He returned to the cruiser, turned around and headed back down the driveway leading away from the mansion. When Gabe looked back in his rearview mirror, Stratford held out his scarred hand to the little girl, who solemnly took it, and they entered the house together.

Gabe shook his head. A strange encounter, to say the

least. He came away from the meeting with more questions than answers. One thing he knew for certain, he'd have to do more digging into the multimillionaire and see if any dirt came up. The man certainly had secrets. But all the same, Gabe doubted he'd found the killer. Strangulation was difficult even with two functional hands—the will to live was a powerful thing, and the victims struggled hard. Those scars on his hand would have made Stratford an unlikely candidate even if his eyes had matched the description Kayla had given.

His mind shifted to Kayla as he passed the lighthouse cottage. He resisted the urge to drop in at the B and B and check on her, knowing his sister would be looking out for her.

On to his next stop—Lawrence Wilson, the hotel developer.

Kayla puttered about the B and B helping in the kitchen to clear away the breakfast dishes, but generally feeling as though she was more in the way than an aid. Dakota had crawled into his bed and still slept.

"At a loose end?" Molly asked, carrying a stack of towels from the laundry room.

Kayla glanced at the sunshine streaming through the window. "I need to get back to the cottage and see the repairman that Gabe called in."

"Jimmy Gaddy?"

"Yes, I think that's the name he gave when we spoke on the phone."

Molly nodded. "I'm not surprised. He's the handyman we use around here. He'll have the doorjamb fixed in no time. What do you need to talk to him about?"

Kayla sighed. "He told me that the lock in the door was weakened by all the strain it took when the doorjamb was broken, so he had to replace it. I need to go pick up the new keys."

"Can't he just leave them for you, maybe in the mailbox?"

Kayla shook her head. "I don't feel safe leaving the keys out where anyone could get to them."

"And I don't feel safe having you go to the cottage by yourself," Molly countered. "I promised Gabe I'd keep you here, where it's safe. He won't like the idea of you driving out there alone. Why don't I send Dakota with you."

"No." Kayla shook her head. "He needs to sleep. The poor boy was up all night with all that was going on. And besides, I won't be there alone. Jimmy will be there when I arrive, and after he leaves, I won't be staying too long, myself. I'm meeting Emma Jenkins for lunch at the marina."

"I suppose that sounds all right." Molly took a couple of steps toward the staircase. "I'll call and tell Gabe that you're heading back to the cottage. He'll want to know."

"Okay." Kayla grabbed her purse, her keys and left the B and B. She felt much more confident driving today. With the roads bathed in sunlight, she'd see any cars closing in on her ready to bounce her off the highway, well before they had a chance. She pulled out her cell phone to call Gabe, but frowned when she saw the battery had died. With everything that had been happening, she must have forgotten to charge it.

"See what I told you about Mommy being absent-minded?" she said with a sigh. "We'll have to add that to our list of things to do when we get home, baby. Meet Jimmy, get the keys, charge the cell phone and use the landline to call Gabe."

Kayla pulled away from the B and B, intent on getting

back to a normal life. Today was a beautiful day, and it gave her back a sense of confidence.

She managed the short drive without incident and the handyman was just finishing up with a coat of paint over the new doorjamb.

Kayla entered the cottage with a feeling of hope. Something about the pungent scent of fresh paint made her optimistic.

"I cleaned up the glass and duct-taped the hole in the window." Jimmy rinsed his paint-covered hands in the kitchen sink. "The replacement glass is on order, but it'll be a couple days before they can ship it from Portland." He collected his tools and stood by the door. "This paint needs to dry before you close the door, and here are your new keys."

Kayla nodded. "Thanks for getting to this so quickly."

"No problem."

"What do I owe you?"

"The bill goes to the real-estate agency renting the cottage. Is there anything else you want me to work on while I'm here?"

Kayla's lips twitched. She wanted to say, *How about rebuilding my confidence*? Instead, she shook her head. "No. That's all that I needed."

"Well, then, I'm off. Remember to let this dry a couple hours before you close it."

"I'll remember."

Once Jimmy left, Kayla plugged her cell phone into the charger, and noticed she had a voice mail.

Emma Jenkins had called to say that she couldn't make their lunch date and to ask if they could make it the next day. Kayla called back and made the arrangements, only slightly disappointed she wouldn't have company for lunch. With bright blue, clear skies, she couldn't be down long.

She gathered her art supplies and easel and headed outside to soak up some sun. Since the door wasn't supposed to be closed until the paint dried, she couldn't barricade herself inside. Besides, the sunshine was calling to her for the first time in a long time, and she needed to air the paint fumes from the house.

"Can't have you sick over paint fumes, can we?" She slid her hand across her belly and smiled, feeling more optimistic than she had in weeks.

She set up her easel far enough away from the edge of the cliffs to be safe and squirted fresh paint onto her palette. The view in front of her was breathtakingly beautiful. To capture the beauty took time and patience, something she normally had a lot of. Since the attack, she'd struggled with unsteady hands, and with her own impatience with herself. Yesterday, she'd been able to paint with Dakota without too much difficulty. She hoped that meant she'd turned a corner.

With a deep breath, she raised her hand, her gaze going to the lighthouse, the cliffs and the sea beyond. As her brush neared the canvas, her hand shook so badly, she almost dropped it.

Frustration filled her.

Why couldn't she do this? Why couldn't she be strong enough to put her trauma behind her and get on with her life?

On the end of that thought an image flashed in her mind of Gabe holding her close, making her feel safe.

Swallowing the sob in her throat, Kayla straightened her shoulders and forced her hand to the canvas. Instead of the scenery in front of her, her brush lifted a pair of blue eyes out of the canvas. Those blue eyes were filled with concern, love and strength.

Her hands steadied, her fingers deftly stroking the white

median. An outline appeared, the face coming to life, complete with laugh lines around the eyes.

With no awareness of the passing time, Kayla painted feverishly, her hand flying over her work, layering shadows, light and color. When her stomach rumbled, reminding her to eat, she stepped back and gasped.

Gabe stared back at her from the canvas, his eyes shining and filled with hope.

"That's amazing."

Kayla spun. So caught up in her work, she hadn't heard the sound of a car or anything else.

A tall gentleman with pitch-black hair and blue eyes stood with his hands tucked in his pockets. He looked vaguely familiar.

Her hand rising to her throat, Kayla fought to catch her breath. "Do I know you?" Her voice shook.

"Probably not, but I know your work." He didn't extend a hand in greeting. "I'm Andrew Stratford. I purchased a number of your paintings at a gallery exhibit a couple weeks ago in Seattle."

The mention of the gallery in Seattle made her stomach flip. "You were there?"

He nodded. "I have one on commission with you now."

"So, you're the buyer." She forced a laugh, fear, like adrenaline, lacing through her. "So many times I don't meet the buyers." Kayla gave him a tight-lipped smile. "H-how did you find me here?"

"Someone mentioned it in town," he answered vaguely. "It occurred to me that I should come out and introduce myself." The man nodded toward the painting behind her. "I met him earlier today. Officer McGregor. He was asking questions about a murder, seemed to think I might be a suspect."

Kayla's stomach bunched. "Are you?"

"A suspect?" He shook his head. "I hope not, and no, I didn't murder the girl." He gave her a hint of a smile for the first time, the gesture making his face less scary and more approachable as he changed the subject. "I like your work, and I want to commission another painting."

Letting out the breath she'd been holding, Kayla managed to laugh. "As long as you're not here to…"

He snorted. "Murder you? Hardly. It would be waste of a good artist."

She inhaled and let the breath out slowly, trying to calm her rampant pulse. "What would you like me to paint?"

His smile faded, his face stone-cold and serious. "A portrait of my daughter."

Kayla hesitated. "I'm not certain I can do it."

"I haven't seen portraits in your portfolio until now, but based on the one you're working on, I'm certain you have the talent to do the job."

Uneasy, standing alone with a stranger, she hedged, "It's just that I don't know if I can channel my talent at this time."

He tipped his head slightly. "Why?"

"I've had some trouble lately and it's made it difficult to paint." Kayla wasn't up to answering this man's questions when she had a million of her own. The most important one was what she needed to do to make him leave. She wasn't comfortable with him there.

Stratford's right hand left his pocket and rose to touch his face. "I know about trouble."

She noticed the scars on the back of his hand and where he'd touched his face and despite how wary she was, Kayla's heart went out to the man for all he'd suffered—the pain of the burns as well as the healing.

"Ms. Davies," he continued, "I also know that the only way to get back to normal is to do the things that you loved in the past until you love them again." He pulled a card from his wallet and handed it to her. "Please consider my offer. I want you to paint a portrait of my daughter."

He didn't wait for her answer, instead he walked away, climbed into his sleek black car and drove away.

Kayla forced air back into her lungs as she stared after him, wondering who the heck Andrew Stratford was, and why he'd really chosen to show up unannounced at her door.

Dakota wheeled his bicycle into the driveway, looking back over his shoulder at the expensive black sedan leaving. "Why did you leave the B and B without telling me, and who was that man?"

Kayla's brows rose. She shook aside her doubts and insecurities and focused on the teen. "Are you my self-appointed keeper?"

Dakota toed his kickstand and leaned the bike on it. "Gabe wanted you to stay at the B and B with Aunt Molly until he was through with his shift."

"Your father isn't my keeper any more than you are and I needed to come home to meet the handyman."

"Whatcha painting?" Dakota looked over his shoulder at the canvas.

Kayla planted her body in front of the canvas. "Nothing. Aren't you early for your lesson? I thought we'd be meeting in the afternoon, after I had lunch with Emma?"

"When I woke up, I found out you'd left the B and B without telling me—and you didn't answer your phone when I tried to call. I wanted to check on you. That's a picture of Gabe, isn't it?" He moved to the side. "Why are you hiding it?"

Why was she? Kayla knew her work expressed her emotions and her feelings. The feelings she had for Gabe McGregor were so new and confusing, she wasn't ready to own up to them yet either in her head or out loud on canvas. But the painting had a way of making them clear as the cloudless sky and that scared her in a completely different way.

Her heart skipped a beat and she had to remind herself to breathe. Based on how she'd painted Gabe McGregor, she could well be on her way to falling for the guy, which would be a big mistake given that he clearly didn't want a commitment. And with her baby on the way, Kayla was a package deal—huge in the commitment department.

Kayla jerked the canvas off the easel and marched toward the house. "Let's get our paintings from yesterday and bring them outside."

"I get it, you don't want to talk about the Gabe painting."

"I don't want to talk about it, and I'd appreciate it if you didn't mention it to your father."

Dakota grinned. "Not a problem." He hauled the second easel out of the cottage and set it up beside hers before he spoke again. "It's a good painting."

Kayla gave the boy a stern look.

He held up his hands in surrender. "Okay, okay. But I don't know why you don't want to talk about your work. You're good. You should sell paintings to people."

She smiled. "I do."

"Would you sell that painting of Gabe to me?"

"I thought you didn't like your father?"

"I don't dislike him." Dakota shrugged. "He grows on you."

Kayla couldn't agree with the kid more. In the past two days, she'd found herself thinking more and more about the police officer—his blue eyes and how strong his hands where when they held her. She cleared her throat and tried to focus on the lesson. "Your father cares about you."

Dakota shrugged. "My mom always said she cared about me, too...until she didn't anymore. I think she got tired of having a kid. One screwup and—" he waved his hand "—here I am in Nowhere, Oregon, with a biological father I didn't know existed five months ago. Who's to say he won't get tired of me, too?"

Her heart squeezed hard at Dakota's story. This kid had been dumped by his mother. She touched her belly, the gentle swell just beginning to make a difference in the way her clothes fit.

How could a mother quit loving her child? "Gabe won't give up on you. He's not that kind of man."

"Yeah. Maybe." He shrugged. "What colors do I mix to get the brownish-blue like the cliffs in the shadows?" Having effectively cut off the conversation about his dad and mother, Dakota kept up a lively stream of conversation for the next hour.

Kayla's belly rumbled as noon approached. When they reached a logical stopping point, she set her brushes down and wiped her hands on a cloth. "I'm hungry, how about you?"

His stomach growled in answer and he smiled sheepishly. "Guess I am, too."

"Why don't we go to town and grab something at the Seaside Café. My treat." Kayla gathered her canvas and palette, carrying them inside.

"I can pay my own way. Besides, I probably owe you for the lessons. I'm sure they don't come cheap." He set his easel on the floor of the living room, propping the canvas against it, studying it with a wrinkled brow. "How much *do* I owe you for the lessons?"

Kayla shook her head. "You don't owe me a thing. In fact, I probably owe you for staying with me last night and today. Let's call it even. Now, are you coming with me, or do I have to eat alone?"

The boy smiled. "I can always put away a hamburger."

"I have no doubt you can. Climb in." She nodded toward the car and turned to lock the door of the cottage, remembering at the last minute that the paint might not be dry. She touched it and her finger didn't stick, so she closed the door and locked it.

The drive to town took ten minutes along the winding roads following the contours of the rocky cliffs lining the cape. When she pulled in to the Seaside Café parking lot, Kayla had trouble finding a spot.

"They're very busy today," she remarked.

"Best food next to Aunt Molly's." Dakota climbed out of the SUV and waited for Kayla on the sidewalk in front of the café. They entered together.

"Hello, Ms. Davies, Dakota, come on in and find yourselves a seat." Nora Taggert waved them toward an empty table in the middle of the room.

Kayla settled into a chair and opened the menu. Dakota didn't bother, declaring he wanted a hamburger, hold the onions.

As Kayla studied the menu, a chill slid across the back of her neck. She felt as if someone was watching her. She made a show of hanging her purse on the back of her chair so that she could turn just enough to look at the other patrons.

A man stood at the cashier's counter, his back to the room. When he turned, Kayla recognized him as Andrew Stratford. His gaze met hers briefly, then he left the building without uttering a word to anyone.

In a booth in the far corner, Jillian Taylor glanced across at Kayla, smiled and waved. Across the table from her sat

Lawrence Wilson, the man Kayla had met the night she'd had dinner at the B and B.

Wilson nodded an acknowledgment, then his attention returned to Jillian. He smiled with the charm of a salesman; Jillian smiled back, her eyes alight, clearly attracted to the man.

Kayla wasn't familiar with any of the other customers in the café and none of them gave her any strange looks other than mild curiosity. She shrugged and looked at her menu, trying to relax.

For a few short hours that day at the cottage, she'd almost felt normal. Painting the portrait of Gabe had been cathartic, liberating, the first step toward replenishing her creative well.

But her conversation with Andrew Stratford and his confession that he'd been at the gallery exhibit the night she'd been attacked had thrown her back to square one of her attempt to conquer her fear.

Now she sat in a diner full of people, and she had no reason to be so anxious.

Or did she?

Chapter 13

Gabe tried Lawrence Wilson's hotel room, but didn't find him there. After reporting in to the police department and kicking off a computer scan through the databases for any information on Andrew Stratford, he stopped by to have a word with the boss.

He marched into Chief Taggert's office. "Anything from the DMV database on Wilson?"

"Got a match on one Lawrence Wilson in Portland, but no priors." The chief pulled up the license photo. The picture matched the man he'd met at the B and B the night before last.

"That's him." Gabe shrugged. "So, he told the truth about being from Portland. Although Portland is only a few hours away from Seattle. He could have been the man who attacked Kayla that night at the gallery. You say he checks out clean?"

The chief nodded. "Not even a traffic fine. Funny thing

is that I did a scan on Lawrence Wilson in the state of Washington at the same time as I did one in Oregon, and look what I found."

Gabe leaned over Chief Taggert's shoulder and stared down at the screen as the chief brought up another photo.

The same Lawrence Wilson stared back at him with a completely different address in Seattle.

Gabe's gut tightened. "You aren't supposed to hold a regular motor vehicle license in more than one state."

"That's the theory. Could be a glitch in the system. The Portland license is newer than the Seattle license. He could have applied and the old one wasn't withdrawn."

"Yeah, but it's worth asking Mr. Wilson about it."

"Agreed," Chief Taggert looked up. "What did you learn from Mr. Stratford?"

"Not much. He claimed he didn't walk as far as the lighthouse two nights ago. Said the fog was too thick, and that he didn't hear a thing."

The chief clicked his pen open and closed. "Doesn't mean he didn't."

"True, but what else do we have to go on?"

"Nothing so far." Taggert clicked the pen again and set it on the desktop. "Could sure use more evidence."

"Anything on the ski mask?" Gabe asked.

"Not yet. I was just about to call the crime lab."

"I'm going to find Wilson and see what I can learn from him."

"You do that. Seems I saw him driving around town with Jillian Taylor. Being that it's lunchtime, they might have stopped for a bite."

"I'll keep that in mind." First, he wanted to check his voice mail and see if he had any responses from the detectives on the earlier cases.

"Don't forget, the FBI agent is scheduled to show up

later today, as long as his flight isn't delayed. Make yourself available, will ya?"

"I will." Gabe sighed. Another long day after a sleepless night at Kayla's. This case had him strung tighter than a violin bow.

The first message on his answering machine was a crank call. The second and third were hang-ups. The fourth caller identified himself as Detective Bryant from Bellingham, Washington. "I'm in the office today. Call me." The fifth message was from a Portland police detective, also asking him to call.

Gabe jerked the phone from its receiver and punched in the Bellingham detective's number, glancing at the clock over the watercooler. Lunchtime. What were the odds the guy was eating at his desk?

After the third ring, Gabe started to hang up, when a voice barked over the line, "Bryant speaking."

Gabe told the man who he was and described the murder in Cape Churn.

"Sounds a lot like our case. The man didn't leave anything in the way of evidence or witnesses. The victim had stepped out her back door to let her dog out when she was abducted and murdered. No one saw it happen. It's been a cold case for the past six months. Hope you find more than we did."

"Any persons of interest that you questioned?"

"A homeless man and a businessman who'd been jogging in the park while visiting the area."

Gabe sat forward. "Businessman? What was his name? What did he look like?"

"Let me check." A long pause ensued. "Les Williams. He checked out clean. No outstanding warrants or abuse charges."

"Any other leads?"

"The victim's sister said that she'd been getting prank phone calls, threatening letters, and someone had been in her house rearranging her jewelry. She said the victim had been afraid to go far from her house because of all the creepy things happening to her."

The same scenario Kayla now lived. Gabe sank back against his chair, his gut knotting. He'd known the cases were similar, but actually hearing the details from someone else made it even more frightening. Even with this detective's description, he felt as though they were no further along than when he'd lifted the phone. "Thanks, Detective Bryant."

"If you learn anything new, let us know. The woman who died was the daughter of a state senator. They still have an outstanding reward out for the arrest and conviction of the murderer."

"I'll let you know." Gabe hung up, scrubbed his hand through his hair and punched the buttons for the Portland police detective.

Expecting a similar outcome, Gabe rolled a pencil across the pad in front of him, his foot tapping the ground between rings.

"Yeah," a voice answered.

"Detective Stanley?"

"That's me." Abrupt was the best way to describe the man's response.

Gabe went through the same description he'd given the Bellingham police detective and got less for his effort. No one had seen anything. The woman had been walking from her building to her car when she'd been abducted and murdered.

"Any DNA evidence?"

"No. The victim was clean. We questioned her ex-boyfriend, but his alibi checked out, even had a witness to back him up."

The Portland case had been the first in the string of red-haired murders six months prior to the one in Cape Churn.

"What's the ex-boyfriend's name?" Gabe asked.

"Rick Watson."

Gabe scribbled the name on the pad, thanked the detective, and promised to pass on any information he might come up with. For now, he had very little to go on.

He booted his computer and logged into the Department of Motor Vehicles in the state of Washington. He keyed in Les Williams and waited for the photo identification to pop up. When it did, he didn't recognize the face. The photo itself wasn't the best quality, blurred just enough to be a problem.

The man in the picture had a neatly trimmed, close-cropped beard and a mustache, and his hair was combed straight back. The description read: hair brown, eyes hazel, height seventy-two inches. Nondescript enough for Gabe to be uncertain if he'd seen him before or not.

Moving on to the case in Portland, he looked up Rick Watson and found a man with dark brown hair hanging over his forehead and down to his collar in the back. He had light brown eyes and stood five feet eleven inches tall. He sported a long mustache but no beard and he wore a diamond stud earring in his right ear.

Gabe ran a scan through the computer for any arrests. One complaint had been filed against him by a former girlfriend, claiming he had tried to choke her when she turned down his marriage proposal. The charge had been dropped before the case made it to court due to death of the alleged victim. The girl ran out into the street and was hit by oncoming traffic a week before the hearing. She'd died instantly.

Knowing he might be grasping at straws, Gabe picked up the phone and dialed Detective Bryant again.

"Bryant."

"This is Officer McGregor. Do you happen to have the address of next of kin for Rick Watson in your file?"

"Let me look." A moment later, Detective Bryant was back. "His only living relative is his mother, who lives in Portland. Martha Watson. But she was no help in the investigation. She didn't know anything."

"Thanks. I appreciate the information." Gabe hung up, tapping his pencil next to Martha Watson's name. On impulse, Gabe enlarged and printed the driver's-license photos for Rick Watson, Les Williams and Lawrence Wilson, cutting out the rest of the license information. He stacked them in a neat pile and picked up the phone again.

Five minutes later, he had an appointment with Martha later that afternoon in Portland, an hour-and-a-half drive from Cape Churn.

He might be chasing his tail, but he had to do something. In the meantime, he wanted to find Lawrence Wilson for questioning, then check on Kayla.

Gabe's groin tightened at the thought of Kayla. The more he saw her, the more he wanted to see her. But he wanted to see her without fear in her beautiful green eyes. And damn it, he would, if it was the last thing he did.

Gabe popped into the chief's office and told him that he'd miss the special agent's arrival and explained why.

Taggert waved him away. "I got it covered. Just go."

When Gabe turned to do just that, the chief hailed him. "Gabe?"

"Yes, sir." He leaned back in the doorway.

"I take it you'll be pulling bodyguard duty at the lighthouse cottage tonight?"

"As soon as I get back to Cape Churn. I shouldn't be later than dinnertime."

"Good luck."

"Thanks." Gabe changed into civilian clothing, left his cruiser at the station and drove through town in his SUV searching for Lawrence Wilson, on the off chance he'd catch sight of the man. When he didn't find him, he stopped at Jillian's real-estate office, where her secretary said the last time she got word from Jillian, she was out showing properties to the man.

They could be almost anywhere and Gabe needed to get on the road. But not before he saw Kayla and made certain she was safe while he went to Portland. He punched in the number for the B and B. Molly answered on the third ring.

"Let me speak with Kayla," Gabe said without preamble.

"She left this morning to go back to the cottage. She said she'd call you and let you know. Guess she didn't," Molly said. "Dakota went over a little later. Haven't heard from either one since."

Gabe sucked in a deep breath and let it out, willing his heart rate to remain natural. The thought of Kayla alone at the cottage made him nervous, even though the killer had limited his assaults to the night. The lighthouse cottage had no other houses close by, which meant anything could happen and no one would know until it was too late. Dakota being there wasn't much more of a relief, considering he was just a boy. Having him there might scare off the murderer by simple safety in numbers, but there was no guarantee. Instead of feeling better, Gabe felt worse. He loved his son and didn't want him hurt standing in the way of a killer.

Gabe stepped on the accelerator and headed south out

of town toward the lighthouse, his pulse increasing with the speed of the vehicle.

He took the turn into the lighthouse driveway too fast, skidding sideways on the gravel. *Calm down.* Everything would be just fine.

Kayla's SUV wasn't parked in front of the house. Dakota's bicycle leaned on its kickstand near the porch. At least he was with Kayla, wherever that could be.

Gabe checked the door, noting the fresh paint. He jiggled the handle, testing the dead bolt. After circling the cottage and peering into the windows, he concluded she'd probably taken Dakota to town. Pulling out his cell phone, he dialed her number. After a moment, he could hear the sound of a phone ringing from inside the house. Gabe shook his head. Kayla had gone off without her phone.

He didn't like not knowing where she was, but the woman had a mind of her own and most likely didn't like being housebound.

A smile curled Gabe's lips. Kayla might be the target of a killer, but she had the guts and chutzpah to carry on with her life. He liked that about her. The woman had spunk.

Ever since he'd walked out on her the night before, he'd regretted leaving. In his heart, he knew Kayla deserved someone who loved her completely, with nothing held back. And deep down, he wanted to love her like that. But was he capable of letting down his guard so completely?

If he was honest with himself, he'd have to admit Kayla scared him. She might be the one he could allow past his guard and into his heart, something Gabe had vowed to never let happen again.

Between Dakota and the red-haired artist, Gabe had started to want things he hadn't dared to want for a very long time. A house, home and family he could love forever.

He couldn't wait to see her again. He needed to apologize, to tell her he'd been wrong. And what? That he wanted to spend the rest of his life with her? That he was willing to let a woman past the wall he'd built since Siena?

His hands tightened on the steering wheel. He'd only known her a couple days. How could these feelings be real?

Back in town, Gabe found Kayla's SUV at the Seaside Café. The tension in his chest loosened as he pulled in to the parking lot. At that moment Kayla exited the café, followed by Dakota.

A light sea breeze caught her green, gold and brown broom skirt, whipping the fabric around her calves, molding it to the curve of her thighs. When she caught sight of Gabe, her face lit with a smile.

Gabe's heart tripped and raced. How did she do that? How did she make him feel like a teenage boy all over again?

Her lips tipped downward and she spoke before he had a chance. "I know you wanted me to stay at the B and B, but I needed to get back to the cottage."

Dakota jumped in. "Gabe, you should see the painting—"

"We're working on during our lesson. It's coming along beautifully," Kayla finished for the boy, placing a hand on his son's arm. "Dakota's got talent."

Dakota's face flushed red and he kicked at the loose gravel in the parking lot. "I've got a long way to go before I'm as good as Kayla."

"We all have to start somewhere." Gabe wanted to say so much more, but now wasn't the time. He could see the boy was taken with Kayla and understood why. She was real, down-to-earth and full of warmth. "Thanks for taking the time to teach him."

"I should be thanking him for keeping me company."

Kayla hooked her arm through Dakota's. "You've got a great kid."

Gabe found himself jealous of how close Kayla was to his own son, but he smiled, glad Dakota had found a productive use of his time. "He never ceases to amaze me. I only wish I'd known him sooner."

"Uh, guys…I'm here, you know. You don't have to talk like I'm not." Dakota pulled free of Kayla's arm and headed for her SUV. "I'll be in the car."

Kayla's gaze followed Dakota, her hand rising to her belly. "He really is a good kid. You're very lucky."

"How are you feeling? The baby giving you any troubles?"

She shook her head. "No. I'm the one who's been giving the baby troubles. All the anxiety and worry can't be good for her."

Gabe smiled. "So you know it's a girl?" His heart swelled with the thought of Kayla holding a baby girl with auburn hair and green eyes just like her mother.

Kayla laughed. "No, I don't go for the sonogram for another two weeks. I just feel like it's a girl. I could be totally wrong."

"She'll be beautiful just like her mother." Gabe reached out and pushed a stray hair off Kayla's cheek.

She looked up at him, her eyes clear, her lips parted slightly.

Gabe had the strongest urge to kiss Kayla, there in the parking lot, in front of God and Cape Churn. His hand dropped to his side and he cleared his throat. "I have to go to Portland this afternoon. I won't be back until late. I'd rather you stayed at the B and B until I get back."

Her brow furrowed. "I want to go back to the cottage and paint while there's daylight."

Gabe glanced at the sky. Sunlight shone down on them,

but in the distance clouds gathered. "There's supposed to be a storm later on, just like last night."

"I'll only stay as long as there's good lighting. Then I'll pack it in and head for the B and B."

"Keep Dakota with you. If anything happens, you'll have backup. He's not a cop, but he can dial 911 just as well as anyone."

Kayla's lips twisted. "You think he'll want to stay and babysit a grown woman?"

Gabe's gaze moved to the boy in the SUV, plugged into his iPod with his head dipping to the beat of the music. "He's happy as long as he has access to his tunes. I have to go. I'm following a lead on the case."

"Then by all means, go." Kayla slipped her purse strap over her shoulder and started for her vehicle.

Gabe fell in step beside her, opening the driver's door for her. "Be careful and aware. I'll be back as soon as possible."

She paused, her hand on the door, her gaze meeting his. "I will." Then she leaned up on tiptoe and aimed a kiss for his cheek.

At the last moment, Gabe turned his face, capturing her lips with his. His hands rose to her hips, pulling her close.

She sighed, leaning into his body, her lips parting slightly.

The kiss deepened, Gabe's tongue sweeping past her teeth to slide alongside hers. She tasted sweet like apple pie and ice cream.

"Seriously?" Dakota called out from inside the SUV. "Haven't you two heard of the no PDA in public rule? It's just not right."

Kayla pushed away from Gabe and dropped into the driver's seat.

Gabe held her door for a moment longer. He wanted

more, but this wasn't the time or the place. "We need to talk."

"Now?" she asked, her brows rising.

"No, later." On impulse, he leaned into the car and pressed another hard kiss to her mouth. "Stay safe."

Her hand rose to her lips. "I will."

Gabe bent to peer around Kayla. "Dakota, take care of her, will ya?"

"Yeah, yeah. Just no kissing around me. Someone might see you."

"I'll make a note of that." Gabe shut the door and stepped back, his gaze following Kayla as she exited the parking lot and headed for the cottage.

"I see how it is," a laughing voice said behind Gabe.

He turned to face Jillian Taylor where she stood on the sidewalk in front of the café.

"No wonder you haven't asked me out on a date."

Lawrence Wilson stood behind her, his lips thin, his eyes narrowed, then he smiled, though the smile seemed forced, his eyes hidden behind sunglasses. "I don't blame the man. Ms. Davies is a very beautiful woman."

Jillian sighed. "Sure, if you prefer red-haired, petite women with boatloads of talent." She slid her arm around Wilson's elbow. "Are you ready to see the lighthouse property?"

Wilson waved his hand. "Lead the way."

Jillian moved toward her car. Lawrence fell in step behind her.

"Mr. Wilson, do you have a minute?" Gabe asked. He needed to get to Portland, but he also needed to talk to this man.

"Why?"

"I have a few questions I'd like to ask."

"Will it take long?" Wilson glanced toward Jillian.

"No."

Wilson waved at Jillian. "Go on, I'll meet you at your building when I'm through with Officer McGregor."

Jillian frowned, her gaze shooting from Lawrence to Gabe. "Is something wrong?"

"No. Not at all." Gabe hoped.

Jillian's ready smile returned. "Okay, then. I'll see you in a few."

After the real-estate agent left, Gabe turned to Lawrence. "Mr. Wilson, I'm leading the investigation into the recent murder."

"Am I a suspect?" Wilson raised his hands. "If so, do I need an attorney?"

"You can consult an attorney if you like, but right now, I just need to know where you were the night before last around midnight."

"I was asleep in my hotel room."

"Can someone at the hotel verify that?"

"I walked by the night clerk on my way up around ten-thirty."

"Mr. Wilson, we ran your name through the Department of Motor Vehicles in Oregon to verify your address."

"Are you sure I'm not a suspect?"

"Frankly, everyone around here is a suspect until we find Rachel Kendrick's murderer."

Wilson nodded. "What about the DMV?"

"And we also ran it through the DMV in Washington and discovered that you have an active driver's license there as well. Can you explain that?"

"How would I know? When I moved to Oregon, I got a new license. They must not have canceled the one in Washington."

"Mr. Wilson, can you tell me where you were two

weeks ago?" Gabe gave him the date of Kayla's assault and waited for the man's response.

"How the hell am I supposed to remember where I was two weeks ago? And what the hell does it have to do with the woman murdered here in Cape Churn? This is sounding more and more like I'm the subject of a witch hunt." His mouth pressed into a tight line. "I'll be glad to answer questions after I've contacted my attorney."

Gabe nodded. "You have that right."

"Does this line of questioning have anything to do with the attack on Ms. Davies?"

Gabe's body grew still. "What attack?" He hadn't mentioned Kayla throughout the interchange and no one outside the police department and his immediate family knew of the connection to the murdered girl and Ms. Davies or the recent vandalism at the lighthouse cottage.

"I listen to the news, I read the papers. Famous artist attacked after gallery showing. It was all over the newspapers a couple weeks ago. I recognized her from the pictures."

Gabe inhaled and let it out. His argument was a reach, but plausible. "Please notify your lawyer. I'll be calling you in to sign a statement."

"Damn right I'm calling my lawyer." Wilson stood straighter, his nostrils flaring. "Are you done?"

"Until you contact that lawyer." Gabe nodded. "Thank you for your time, Mr. Wilson."

Lawrence Wilson snorted and walked away.

Gabe watched him as he climbed into his BMW and drove away.

His gut told him Lawrence Wilson was one to watch. Gabe patted the photographs in his pocket, climbed into his cruiser and drove out of town, more determined than ever to find the murderer, and soon. If the killer thought Gabe was on to him, he might stop teasing and get serious about killing.

Chapter 14

Kayla hauled her easel and paints back out of the cottage and worked all afternoon. Painting Gabe had given her the courage and inspiration to move on to her contracted work.

Jillian and Mr. Wilson had come, viewed the cottage and lighthouse and left, without bothering Kayla or Dakota.

As Kayla worked, Dakota alternated between working on his painting, sitting on the porch, wandering around the cottage and napping on the sofa in the living room. Around four o'clock in the afternoon, he'd made several passes around the house, looking more and more caged with each lap.

The constant movement distracted Kayla. Finally, she put down her paintbrush and palette and intercepted Dakota's latest circle. "Go home, Dakota."

"Why? I thought you liked having me here." His hurt,

puppy-dog look almost made Kayla reconsider her request for him to leave.

"I do like having you around, but you need to go. The more you move the less I paint."

He hunched his shoulders. "Sorry. I promise to sit still."

"No. I want you to go home. I figure I have about two more hours of daylight if the clouds don't take over first. I'll quit while there's still plenty of light and be at the bed-and-breakfast before dark."

"But Gabe wanted me to watch out for you."

"And I'm telling you, I can manage on my own. No one is going to attack me during the daylight hours, and I'll head over to the B and B before long, anyway." She smiled. "Now, go."

Dakota's brows dipped low. "Well, if you're sure."

"Positive."

He kicked the stand and climbed onto his bike. "Call me if you need me."

"I will." She smiled and waved as Dakota rode his bike down the driveway.

Once he was out of sight, second thoughts plagued her. Alone at a remote cottage…

She shivered and returned to her easel, determined to take up where she'd left off. "If I'm not going to let myself be afraid of shadows anymore, then I *definitely* shouldn't be afraid of sunlight," she informed her baby.

At first the tremors slowed her down, but she thought about Gabe and the way she felt when he held her in his arms. Soon the shakes disappeared.

The view drew her in, her hand flying over the palette and canvas, painting the dark, shadowy cliffs with the smoky clouds roiling in the distance, their edges gilded by sunlight. White-capped waves smashed against the base of the rock face, splashing upward in a breathtaking display of nature.

Having completed the clouds, Kayla became so immersed in capturing the waves, she didn't look up until wind buffeted the canvas, tipping the easel.

She steadied the painting, and for the first time in hours noticed how stormy the skies had grown.

Gathering her painting and palette, she hurried inside, making a return trip for the easel as the first drops of rain pelted the ground. Without much warning, the skies opened, dumping buckets of rain on her.

By the time she reached the porch, she was soaked to the skin. Inside, she locked the door and stripped to her underwear to avoid trailing water through the house. She gathered her wet clothing, carried it to the laundry room and then ducked into the bathroom for a shower.

As the warm water sluiced over her body, her thoughts drifted once more to Officer McGregor and that soul-stealing kiss outside the café. What had he meant by that kiss? Anything? And what could he possibly have to talk to her about? He'd made it clear he didn't think being with her was a good idea.

Hope filled her heart, and her body tingled all over in anticipation of his return. Her common sense argued that she had no business getting involved with Gabe when he was clearly not ready for a relationship. But if he was willing to give it a try… She certainly wasn't going to say no out of hand. Lord knew, she had issues of her own. If he could be patient with hers, she could be patient with his—as long as he was willing to put in the effort.

As she soaped her body, she couldn't shut out the memory of Gabe's laughing blue eyes and his warm, gentle hands. She recalled how it felt to have him apply the soap to her skin, to stand beneath the water with him, naked, their bodies raging with desire.

Heat rose from her core, sending sizzling shocks of energy through her system. She hadn't felt this way since… well, since the last time she and Gabe had made love.

She tried to count off her raging desire to the increased hormones, but it wasn't just that.

Gabe was the kind of man every woman dreamed of. Kind and sexy, he was warm and caring, trying to create a life with a son he'd never known. Patient, tender, understanding, yet firm, he made a great father to the teen. How would he be with a newborn? Would he ever let a woman into his life long enough to marry and have more children? Could he accept another man's child as his own? Was it fair of her to expect him to?

Kayla turned down the heat on the water until it chilled her skin, dousing her inner burning. She might never find out. Just because he'd kissed her in the parking lot didn't mean he'd changed his mind about making love to her again.

The clock on her nightstand blinked a bright green seven o'clock. Gabe had said he'd be back late. With the rain pouring down, his travel time from Portland would lengthen considerably. Kayla strode to the picture window, the duct tape holding back the rain like a giant Band-Aid on the jagged glass.

Rain slashed against the cottage as viciously as the night before. Kayla had no desire to venture out on the road and risk running her vehicle over a cliff. As dark and stormy as it was outside, that was a distinct possibility. Though she'd promised Gabe she'd head to the B and B, she knew he'd understand if she didn't. Maybe the rain would slow down soon, and she could try driving then.

Having showered and changed into clean, dry clothing,

she didn't want to go back out and get drenched all over again. Instead, she made a sandwich and sat at the table, wishing she had someone to talk to in order to pass the time until Gabe arrived. She called Molly and let her know she wasn't going to get out in the rain, that she'd stay at the cottage until the weather cleared.

Halfway through her sandwich, she picked up her plate and set it in the sink. The excitement of the previous night and the baby growing inside had sapped her energy. No longer hungry and too sleepy to care, she propped the painting of Gabe on the coffee table, blocking the view of the dark picture window. She lay on the sofa, drawing a light blanket over herself.

Going to sleep might not be a good idea, but she'd gotten so little of it lately, surely just a few minutes of shut-eye before Gabe arrived wouldn't put her in too much danger.

With Gabe's shining eyes watching over her, making her feel warm and safe, she drifted off to sleep.

Gabe arrived in Portland well before the scheduled time to meet with Martha Watson, Rick Watson's mother. He pulled to the side of the road and called the number the detective had given him for the sister of the first victim, Nancy Smith. He arranged for a place to meet and hung up with fifteen minutes to get across town in traffic.

He arrived at the designated coffee shop and entered, expecting to find a woman with red hair. Instead, a brunette stood when he walked in the door.

"Are you Officer McGregor?" The woman extended her hand. "I'm Briana Smith, Nancy's sister."

"Thanks for meeting with me on such short notice."

"I'm just glad someone is working on the case. It's been

so long." She waved toward a table with a cup of coffee sitting on it. "Have a seat."

"I apologize. I don't have a lot of time. I just wanted to find out what you knew about your sister's murder."

Briana's eyes closed, her lips tightening. "She should still be alive today. If any of us had been paying attention, she would be. The signs were all there."

"You can't undo the past or second-guess yourself. It's self-defeating."

The brunette nodded. "I know all that. I just can't help but think I could have done something to stop it."

"Tell me."

"About six weeks before..." Briana paused, swallowed hard and continued, "She started dating a guy from Tacoma, Washington. A long-distance relationship that seemed to be going well, until she got a promotion and her work demanded more of her time. When she realized the distance was going to be a problem, she broke it off with Rick—that's his name, Rick Watson. The breakup was all nice and civil. The next week she started getting prank calls, graffiti on her apartment walls and car. The calls were from public places or untraceable phones."

"Did she report it to the police?"

"Yes. She was scared. The graffiti was threatening." Briana stared at Gabe. "I saw it. It scared me, too. But I was too wrapped up in my own job and life. I should have made her move in with me. One night she had to work late."

Gabe sat silent, waiting for Briana to continue when she pulled herself together.

"She was walking to her car in the parking lot, talking on her cell phone to me." Tears filled Briana's eyes. "I should have told her to get someone to walk her out. But I just didn't think... I heard her scream, then she dropped the phone." Her head shook slowly back and forth. "I called the police, but they couldn't get to her in time."

His chest tight, his pulse speeding, Gabe reached across the table and rested his hand on Briana's.

"He tossed her body in a Dumpster like she was some kind of trash." The tears slipped from her eyes, trickling down her cheeks. "The bastard needs to die some really horrible death."

"Did anyone follow up with the ex-boyfriend?"

"The police questioned him, but he had witnesses who said he was in Tacoma the night my sister died. The police couldn't find the killer, so the case has been languishing." Her hand turned to grip his. "Tell me you'll get him. Please. My sister deserves justice."

"I'll do my best." His fingers tightened around hers. "Do you have a photo of your sister's boyfriend?"

Briana pulled her phone from her purse. "The only one I have is a picture she texted to me of the two of them. The image isn't clear, so you can't really see what he looks like." She touched a few buttons and flipped through the screens, stopping on one of a woman with red hair and pale skin. The quality of the picture wasn't sufficient to indicate her eye color, but the police report had indicated Nancy Smith had green eyes.

The man standing behind her had either dark blond or light brown hair, hanging down past his collar, slicked back from his forehead. He sported a pair of mirrored sunglasses, completely hiding his eyes. The picture wasn't anything he could take to court, even if the boyfriend was the man who'd killed Nancy.

A glance at his watch had Gabe pushing back in his chair. "Ms. Smith, thank you for your time. I'll get back to you once we know more."

She caught his arm with a desperate grip. "Catch him."

"I'll do my best." As he drove to Mrs. Watson's house, Gabe reflected on what Briana had said about the killer leaving messages. It was the same scenario as that in Cape Churn. What were the odds? It had to be the same guy.

When he arrived at Mrs. Watson's, he climbed her porch steps, still lost in thought, and knocked on the door.

Mrs. Watson lived in a small, two-story house in an older neighborhood of Portland. The building appeared to date back to the early 1930s, the wood planks on the porch thick with many layers of paint, the top coat peeling in places.

Glancing at his watch, Gabe knocked again. If he didn't hurry, it'd be way past dark before he returned to Cape Churn. He couldn't be much later, not with Kayla exposed and at risk of another attack from a crazy man.

The curtain moved in the front window and a wrinkled face peered out. A few moments later, the locks clicked and the door swung open.

"You must be Officer McGregor." She held the door wide. "Please, come in."

"Thank you, ma'am." Gabe stepped inside. A long, narrow hallway stretched before him with doors opening off each side and a staircase rising up to his left. "I'm sorry, I arrived early, but there's a storm coming and I need to get back to Cape Churn before it breaks."

"That's quite all right." She shuffled through the doorway to their right and waved at a faded sofa, whose floral pattern had seen better days. "Please, sit down. Can I get you something to drink?"

"No, thank you." He patted his pocket, anxious to show the photos to the woman, but wanting to ease into the discussion about her son. "Ma'am, I wanted to discuss your son, Rick, and his girlfriend."

The woman shook her head, her eyes sad. "What a terrible tragedy, Nancy's death. You know, they never found her murderer."

Gabe nodded. "That's what I understand. I'd like to know more about her relationship with Rick. Do you remember?"

"As if it was yesterday." Martha stared toward a curtained window as if she could see beyond the fabric. "Rick was so in love with Nancy. I thought the two of them would be married and having babies by now. I so want grandchildren before I die. You see, I had Rick late in life and his father died when Rick was only three." Martha blinked and looked across at Gabe. "What was your question?"

"I wanted to know about Rick and Nancy's relationship."

"Oh, yes." She glanced down at her hands. "Rick loved Nancy so much he wanted to marry her. He proposed and she turned him down." Martha looked up, her eyes glassy with tears.

"Did she say why?"

"She said she wasn't ready." A tear slipped down the old woman's cheek. "Rick found out she'd been seeing someone else. Such an ugly situation. Poor Rick was beside himself."

"What did he do?"

"Nancy told the police he tried to choke her. They arrested him and let my son out on bail with a restraining order against him. He couldn't get within one hundred yards of Nancy." Martha shook her head again, staring at the rug. "My Rick wouldn't hurt a fly. He's always been so kind and gentle. Such a good little boy when the bullies weren't picking on him."

"Bullies?" Gabe prompted.

"Oh, growing up, the bullies picked on him since he didn't have a father. Teased him for being a mama's boy."

Mrs. Watson frowned. "Nothing wrong with loving your mother, is what I said."

"What happened to Nancy?"

The woman looked up and blinked, then shook her head. "Terrible tragedy. She ran out in front of oncoming traffic just a week before the trial. Died instantly." Martha sighed. "Rick was so upset, he couldn't make it to the funeral." The woman wiped a tear from her eye. "That was six months ago. I don't think Rick ever really got over Nancy." She rose and walked to the mantel over the fireplace and lifted a photo of a young couple. "This is Nancy and Rick before they broke up."

Gabe stared down at a pretty auburn-haired woman with pale skin and green eyes. She smiled into the camera, happy, pretty and full of life. His breath lodged in his throat. God, she looked a lot like Kayla. The man beside her had longish brown hair and a mustache.

"Mrs. Watson—" Gabe pulled the photos from his front pocket and held out the one of Rick Watson's mug shot first "—is this a photo of your son?"

"Why, yes. Oh, but that picture was awful. The one they took at the police station. He doesn't look anything like that now."

"What about these photos? Do you recognize the man in them?" Gabe held out the photo of Lawrence Wilson from his Washington and Oregon driver's licenses.

She tipped her glasses down to the end of her nose and studied the pictures, a smile crossing her face. "That's much better. Rick sure cleaned up nicely, didn't he?"

For a very long moment, Gabe couldn't breathe, couldn't speak, couldn't move.

The old woman glanced up at Gabe, smiling, her eyes alight. "He was here to see me two weeks ago. He stopped in on his way back from a trip to Seattle and stayed a whole week." She pointed to a photo of Lawrence Wilson. "I don't have a recent picture of my son. Do you mind if I have that one?"

Sucking in a deep breath, Gabe handed the woman all the photos and stood. "Thank you, Mrs. Watson. I regret the need to rush out, but I have to be back to work in Cape Churn as soon as possible." Sooner than possible.

Gabe left Mrs. Watson's house, leaped off the steps and ran for his vehicle. Damn. Rick Watson was Lawrence Wilson, and he was running free in Cape Churn.

Just because Lawrence and Rick were the same person didn't make him the murderer, Gabe argued with himself. But the fact that he'd attempted to strangle his girlfriend added more credence to jumping to that conclusion. Add that to the fact he'd lived in Washington prior to moving back to Oregon, and that he clearly shared the killer's interest in redheaded women, and it was too much coincidence to be far-fetched.

As soon as he climbed into his SUV, he hit the speed-dial button for Chief Taggert's office. When he got Taggert's answering machine, he dialed Taggert's cell phone. The line went directly to voice mail, indicating the man was either on his phone or out of range.

Damn! Gabe hung up and dialed Kayla's home phone number.

The line rang and rang, and finally rolled over to the answering machine. "Kayla, if you get this message before I get back, don't let Lawrence Wilson in the cottage or anywhere near you. I think he's the killer. If he comes anywhere near the house, call the police. I'm on my way back from Portland."

He dialed her cell phone. Still no answer. He left the same message, his frustration mounting.

Gabe hit the off button, the urge to throw the cell phone

so strong he almost flung it out the window. What was the use of cell phones when you got so little reception outside of Cape Churn?

He dialed the B and B landline. As soon as his sister picked up, he dived in, "Molly, where's Kayla?"

"What, no hello?" Molly laughed. "She's at the lighthouse cottage. She never came to the B and B."

"She what?" His heart slammed into his ribs.

"Dakota came back without her around four. Kayla sent him home saying she'd pack it in before dark and come over. Well, it started raining before dark and she called to say she was fine, and that she didn't want to get out in the rain. Do you want me to go over there?"

"No, and keep Dakota from going as well. I'll have the police department send someone to keep an eye on her."

"Is she in danger?"

"Maybe. I can't get hold of her. I'm going to send over the police."

"Oh, dear, now you've got me really scared for her. I'll call the police myself."

"No, let me. I need to talk with the chief anyway to let him know what's going on." Gabe hung up. He had to get through to the chief and let him know what suspicions he had. If Lawrence Wilson truly was the killer, Jillian could be in trouble as well.

A loud boom startled Kayla out of sleep so suddenly that she fell from the couch onto the floor. She landed with a thump, the breath knocked from her lungs. For a moment she lay staring up at the coffee table, the sofa and the ceiling, wondering where the hell she was.

Two more reverberating booms shook the cottage again and Kayla jumped to her feet, ready to run out of the house, fearing an earthquake. She ran to the window and stared out past the duct-taped patch into nothingness. The rain had stopped and once again the Devil's Shroud had slipped over the land, softening hard edges and obliterating the view of the ocean. She felt as if the cottage had been wrapped in a huge woolly blanket, smothering tight against the woodwork.

Kayla glanced at the clock on the wall. Only eight-thirty. She'd been asleep for over an hour. Maybe Molly could tell her what the booming had been. She picked up the phone and dialed the number she had scribbled on a piece of paper.

Not until she pressed the phone to her ear did she realize there was no dial tone. She set the phone on the cradle and dug in her purse for her cell phone. When she glanced down at the bars, she knew it was useless. The No Service message was displayed on the screen.

A pale beam of light glowed in the side window, the light pushing through the fog, moving toward her from the direction of the driveway. "Gabe?" She ran to the door and flung it open, peering out into the night. More booming came from the direction of town, not that she could see anything through the fog. She couldn't even see the vehicle headed her way, just a growing glob of light getting bigger the closer it came.

What if it wasn't Gabe?

As quickly as she had opened the door, she closed it and slammed the newly fixed dead bolt home. She leaned her head toward the window and tried to see who was coming up the driveway.

A shape of a dark sedan barely materialized out of the fog and pulled to a halt in the gravel. A door opened and a man's tall figure climbed out the driver's side.

Kayla's heart fluttered in her throat as her fingers clutched the curtains.

The passenger door opened and another figure emerged, not as tall, and thinner. As the pair moved toward the door, Kayla backed away from the window, inch by inch.

The porch light shone down as far as the steps, making the world hazy and muted. A light laugh, muffled by the window glass, floated through to Kayla, and Jillian Taylor mounted the steps, shining a flashlight behind her....

At Lawrence Wilson, the resort developer.

Kayla nearly fainted from relief. When Jillian knocked at the door, she jerked it open before she could knock a second time.

"Kayla, honey. Sorry to bother you so late, but Lawrence dropped by before I could get out of my office and insisted on seeing the cottage one more time. He heads back to Portland tomorrow. The fog didn't seem as bad in town, but once we got on the highway, well, it's crazy out there."

"I can't believe you made it this far. I can't see off the end of the porch."

Jillian shifted a strand of her straight blond hair behind her ear. "Did you hear a noise a few minutes ago? I wasn't sure. We had the music up a little loud. I couldn't tell if it was thunder or the sound of the bass guitar."

"I thought I did hear something. It sounded like it came from town."

"Hmm. Wonder what it was about." She turned to Lawrence. "Maybe we should head back."

"We can't see two feet in front of us out on the road. It's too dangerous," Lawrence said. "Perhaps we could wait a few minutes here and see if the fog lifts a little before we attempt the road again."

Somewhat glad for the company, Kayla held open the door. "It is too dangerous to be driving along the highway in this. Please. Come in." She stood to the side as Jillian and Lawrence entered, wiping their wet shoes on the welcome mat.

"I should be used to this by now, but the fog seems thicker than normal these last few days." Jillian shrugged out of her jacket and hung it on a hook on the wall. "Do you mind if I use your bathroom?"

"Not at all, you know where it is." Kayla pointed toward the bedroom and followed Jillian's progress until she stood alone in the living room with Lawrence Wilson.

She turned to the man and tried to smile, but when she glanced up at him, he was staring down at her, his eyes narrow, his mouth tipped up at one corner in what Kayla could only classify as a snarling smirk. She noticed he wasn't wearing his sunglasses tonight, and without them, she could see his eyes clearly. There was something disturbingly familiar about them....

A chill stimulated by the cool fog outside shook Kayla's frame. "Seems like a bad day to be looking at property. You're not going to see much."

"The reverse is true as well." He spoke in a low, gravelly whisper.

Kayla wasn't sure she'd heard him correctly. "What did you say?" she asked.

"What happened to the word on the window?"

"What word?" Kayla took a step backward, the contents of her belly flipping cartwheels.

Lawrence smiled, his light brown gaze holding hers. He reached out to touch the necklace she wore, his fingers brushing the base of her throat. "Where's the locket?"

Fear rushed over her, flooding her senses in an overpowering surge. Her entire body shook all the way out to her tingling fingers. "You..."

His smile widened, his eyes narrowing. "Loved your artwork in Seattle."

All the helpless rage and desperation she'd experienced while this man had choked her bubbled up inside her, spurring her to action. "Jillian!"

The bathroom door burst open and Jillian ran through the bedroom. "What? What's wrong, Kayla?" She turned to Lawrence. "What happened?"

Kayla backed away another step, her fingers reaching for the phone on the counter. "It's him." She pointed at Wilson. "He's Rachel Kendrick's murderer. He's the man who attacked me in Seattle. Oh, God, it's him." Her gaze blurring, she fumbled to key the emergency number.

With a look of utter innocence, Lawrence stepped up beside Jillian. "I have no idea what she's talking about." He swept his hand to the side. "Do I look like I'd murder a woman?"

He sounded so sane, so calm and sensible. It made the sinister gleam in his eyes even more frightening. Kayla's fingers found the buttons she needed and she hit Talk.

The line remained dead.

Lawrence laughed. "What? No service?"

Jillian's brows drew together and she moved toward Kayla. "I don't understand. Why did you call Mr. Wilson a murderer?"

"Because he is." Kayla grabbed Jillian's hand and pushed her behind her, inching her toward the door. With her other hand, she snatched the can of wasp spray Gabe had left on the countertop. "Run, Jillian," she urged. "Run for help. He's crazy. He likes to scare his victims then strangle them."

Jillian planted her feet and refused to move. "What are you talking about? Lawrence? Do you have any idea?"

Lawrence's gaze narrowed, his lips thinning, his hand reaching beneath his jacket. "She's a whore."

Kayla raised the can of spray, aimed it at Lawrence's face and pressed the button.

At the same time, Lawrence yanked a pistol from beneath his jacket.

The spray hit him full in the face and he screamed.

Kayla threw herself at Jillian, knocking her through the open door and out onto the porch. "Run, damn it!"

A loud bang blasted her eardrums at the same time something slammed into her right shoulder, flinging her forward. Kayla tumbled off the deck onto the soaked ground, her head spinning, her mind telling her to get up, run, save her baby. But her body refused to cooperate.

She tried to push to her feet, but the heels of her bare feet slipped on the damp grass and her right arm wouldn't work. She rolled over and pushed up with her left hand, scrambling to her feet.

Jillian flew off the porch and landed beside her. "Kayla, oh, God, Kayla." Using her left arm, Kayla grabbed Jillian and stumbled to the side of the house, out of sight and range of the pistol.

"Run, Jillian, go for the road, get help. Hurry. Stay low in the fog, follow the gravel." Kayla pushed her away from her.

"What about you? I can't leave you with him."

"Yes. You. Can. I won't get far. You can." She shoved in the direction she knew the road would be. "Now go."

A sobbing Jillian staggered away in her high heels, disappearing into the fog.

Footsteps stomped onto the porch and an angry roar blasted through the fog. "I'll kill you, bitch."

Shooting pain radiated through her arm, making her dizzy, but she couldn't give up. Her baby depended on her to stay alive. Not wanting to follow Jillian and put her in the line of fire, Kayla turned the opposite direction, stumbling into the murky night, nearly tripping on the can of wasp spray. She snatched it from the ground, the effort costing her as her head reeled and her vision blurred.

Concentrating on keeping her balance, she straightened and pushed through the fog as fast as she could without running face-first into a tree, the cottage or the edge of the cliff. Her foot caught on a rock and she fell to her knees, jolting her arm, sending another wave of pain shooting through her shoulder. She clamped down hard on her lip to keep from crying out.

"You can't hide from me. I will find you, just like I found you here. Thought you were so smart leaving Seattle." He laughed, the sound more chilling than the air. "*I* sent that brochure for Cape Churn. What you don't understand is that you're mine and always will be. Until death do us part."

His voice grew closer.

Kayla lurched to her feet, swayed and straightened, her vision fuzzy as she ran into the fog.

A shot rang out, the sound loud, as if echoing off the descended clouds. Hot liquid ran down her arm, dripping off her fingertips. She was losing blood, but she'd lose her life if she didn't get away from Lawrence.

I want my baby to live. She repeated the mantra over and over, the instinct to survive pushing her feet forward. A large structure loomed out of the fog so suddenly Kayla almost smacked right into it. The lighthouse.

She rounded the side of the building, found the door and dropped the can of spray. When she'd given her the information about the cottage, Jillian had told her all about the lighthouse. Where had she said that key was? On her hands and knees, Kayla felt around the steps and the area beside the steps until she located a large stone, remembering Jillian's instructions. A skeleton key lay beneath the stone, should she feel like climbing the tower.

Kayla fumbled for the skeleton key beneath the stone, her hand patting the cool, damp earth until her fingers curled around the long, metal key. She lurched to her feet, and fitted it into the door with her left hand.

The pounding of feet on gravel behind her made her hand shake.

Lawrence had obviously found the path and was headed her way.

Sobs rose in her throat as she pushed the key into the lock. Her fingers fumbled and the key fell to the ground with a metallic clatter.

"Nancy, you don't love him, you love me. You're mine. I'll never let him have you." Lawrence's disembodied voice floated toward her as if in a nightmare, the faceless villain lurking in the mist.

Kayla dropped to her knees and groped for the key, her left hand less maneuverable than her right. She found it, rose, swayed and jammed the key into the lock. At first it wouldn't turn, the rusty mechanism stiff with disuse. She wiggled the key and tried again, desperation making her hold slip on the rusty key.

At last the lock clicked. She twisted the knob, pushed open the door, grabbed the can of wasp spray and ran into the lighthouse building, slamming shut the door behind her.

Complete darkness surrounded her as she felt for the dead bolt, fitted the key into it and locked it from the inside to keep Lawrence out.

No sooner had she pulled the key free than something hit the door with such force it shook. "Nancy!" Lawrence raged, his voice high-pitched, the fury palpable. Fists pummeled the door, rattling the ancient, corroded lock. Then silence.

Kayla backed away until her ankles bumped against the steps leading to the top.

A thunderous bang reverberated off the walls. A tiny object whizzed past her injured arm and hit the wall beside her hip. Splinters flew through the air, spearing her legs.

He was shooting at the lock. It wouldn't be long before he destroyed it and he'd be inside.

Too late, Kayla realized that she had trapped herself inside the lighthouse with no way to escape. Her only hope lay in the knowledge that the police made an hourly patrol by her cottage. Plus, Gabe had promised to come by when he got back from Portland. Hopefully someone would notice something amiss or find Jillian wandering the highway.

Moving in pitch-black, Kayla couldn't tell up from down, right from left. She tapped the steps with the toe of her shoe, leaned the good hand clasping the can on the wall and climbed the steps leading to the top, praying someone would come soon.

Below, another bang blasted the air and a loud crash indicated the door had slammed inward.

Her breath coming in ragged gasps, Kayla raced up the winding metal stairs, climbing higher and higher up the lighthouse tower.

Please, Gabe, she prayed silently. *Get here soon.*

Chapter 15

Gabe sped through the night toward Cape Churn, his body leaning forward as if he could see better the nearer he was to the windshield. The closer he got to the town, the thicker the Devil's Shroud grew until he crept along, dodging cars going slower than his. Too many close calls and near misses had his body so tense he could barely push air through his lungs.

He had to get to Kayla. His gut told him she was in trouble and nothing would stop him from getting there short of driving off the cliff highway.

When he neared Cape Churn, he dialed the police station. No one answered. The fog glowed pale orange in a huge halo over the buildings, brightening as he drew nearer. When he passed the first few houses on the outskirts he could make out flames rising into the night, the light reflecting off the fog illuminating the town center and the chaos all around.

Heart thumping, his hands gripping the wheel, he pulled to a stop next to a man standing in the road, barefoot, wearing pajamas. "What happened?"

"It's crazy." The man shoved a hand through his hair and shook his head. "An explosion knocked me out of my bed… When I came out to see what was going on, I saw flames. I'm not sure, but I think something exploded on Main Street."

Gabe thanked him and pushed on, driving slowly through the streets filled with people now running toward the source of the flames.

As Gabe rounded the corner of the bank building, his heart skidded to a halt, his foot hitting the brake.

Where the police station had been, there now rose a raging inferno. He slammed his SUV into Park, jumped out and raced toward the building.

Fire trucks lined the street, full-time and volunteer firefighters aimed hoses at the center of the burning mass. Gabe ran past townspeople gaping at the turmoil. When he spotted the fire chief, he raced toward him. The chief of police stood beside the fire chief, his face grave.

Gabe slid to a halt on the damp pavement beside Taggert. "What happened?"

"Thank God you're back." The police chief nodded to the charred remains of a hunk of metal in front of the crumbled station. "Someone parked a truck beside the station and it blew up. Not sure who or why."

"Damn." Gabe stared at the station, the inferno still blazing as the firefighters did their best to confine it to just one building. "Did you get everyone out?"

Taggert nodded. "We did. The dispatcher, Gene Ledbetter, should be at the hospital by now. Looked bad, but the EMTs think he'll pull through. The desk sergeant received lacerations and suffered from smoke inhalation, but he'll make it as well. Everyone else was on patrol and it was a slow night for the jail cells. Thank the Lord they were empty and the FBI agent didn't make it down from Seattle."

Gabe breathed a sigh, his jaw clenching. "Who would have done this?"

"I don't know, but everyone is helping out. We're short on communication, with the main emergency lines burning."

Which explained why Gabe hadn't been able to get through to the police station. "Chief, I tried to get through to you on my way back to Cape Churn."

"That's right. How'd the interview with the Watson woman go?"

"She recognized some photos I brought with me as those of her son."

"Photos?" The chief turned away from the fire, his full attention on Gabe. "What photos?"

"I enlarged the driver's-license photos of Lawrence Wilson, both from the Washington DMV and the Oregon DMV, without the data associated with the licenses themselves." Gabe stared at the chief. "She identified both as her son, Rick Watson."

The chief swore. "And I had hoped we wouldn't have any trouble tonight, given we're pretty much out of business."

Gabe's stomach flipped, his pulse kicking into high gear. "No one can get a call in to 911?"

"Nope."

And the patrols were probably here in town helping out with the fire. If Kayla hadn't gone to the B and B after the rain stopped, she was on her own in the lighthouse cottage.

"I have to get to Kayla."

The chief's eyes widened. "You don't think…"

"I hope not."

"Get out there. I'll send a message over my car radio for the night-shift patrols to make their way out to the lighthouse. You might need backup."

Gabe ran back to his vehicle, jumped in and weaved through the bystanders on his way south, out of town.

His cell phone rang beside him on the seat. He snatched it up, praying it was Kayla. The number to the B and B flashed across the screen. He hit the talk button and pressed the phone to his ear.

"Gabe? What the hell's going on?" Molly's anxious voice filled his ear.

His hands tightened on the wheel, dread filling every cell in his body. "What do you mean?"

"A few minutes ago, a boom shook the walls. I was in the shower and thought at first it was an earthquake. But when I came out, the Johnsons assured me it was more like an explosion."

"It *was* an explosion—someone blew up the police station."

"Oh, Lord, is everyone all right?"

"They're fine. You're okay? No damage from the explosion?"

"No, no damage, but when I looked around for Dakota after I got out of the shower, he was gone."

"How long ago?"

"I wasn't in the shower more than fifteen minutes. I told him to stay put, but he was really worried about Kayla. He was practically crawling the walls with his pacing. I didn't think he'd leave or I would have watched him more closely."

"He's on his way to her cottage."

"God, Gabe, the fog is awful out here. If he's not careful, he could run his bicycle off the road…" Her voice faded.

She didn't say it, but Gabe could imagine she worried the boy would get going too fast on the slick roads and run off one of the drop-offs on the highway between the B and B and Kayla's cottage.

Adrenaline spiked in Gabe's veins as he pulled onto the road leading to the lighthouse. He increased his speed, despite the insanely thick fog rising up like a wall, blinding his every move. Several times he narrowly missed hitting the guardrails lining the most dangerous drop-offs along the coastal highway. His foot eased off the accelerator. No matter how fast he wanted to go, he could only go as fast as the conditions would allow. He'd be of no use to Kayla and Dakota if he ran his SUV off a cliff into the ocean.

The ten-minute drive out to the lighthouse cottage passed like a slow-motion movie. Negotiating the road in near-zero visibility, Gabe had time to think.

Four months ago, he'd been living in Seattle, doing the job he was born to do. Police work, protecting the innocent, bringing the guilty to justice. He'd lived each day carefree of commitment, no one to answer to, no one to worry about. The women in his life hadn't been an issue because he didn't let them close enough.

Until Siena had dropped Dakota at his apartment doorstep, reminding him that Gabe McGregor wasn't alone in the world and that others depended on him for more than the cop he was. His son's entry into his life had made him responsible for another person's happiness and shown him that being there for a loved one wasn't a bad thing.

Dakota had taught him that in the few short months he'd known his son. No matter how hard it was to get through to the kid, Gabe couldn't forget that Dakota depended on him to nurture, love and protect.

His son's teenage insolence and sullen behavior had been tempered by his passion for art, his love for his aunt Molly, his occasional tolerance for the dad he'd never known and his desire to help others in need.

And despite the hardships, Gabe had started looking forward to spending time with his son, getting to know him and what made him happy. His son had taught him to love again. Not only that, but their move to Cape Churn had helped Gabe reestablish his connection with his only sibling, Molly. For these things Gabe could be grateful.

Dakota most likely had been the catalyst for Gabe opening his heart to love for others. By asking Dakota to trust that his father wouldn't leave him, Gabe had been forced to come to grips with his own distrust of the ones he loved leaving, the distrust that had been rooted in Siena's betrayal. Dakota had needed to learn that not all parents were the same. Gabe had needed to learn that not all women were the same.

But it wasn't just Dakota. Gabe had to meet the right woman. One who could mean more to him than just a casual affair. One who could share his life and the love he felt for his home. A woman willing to love him and his family, the people he held most dear. A woman who shared his passions and wasn't afraid to trust herself to his care and possibly love him in return.

For the first time since he was a teen, Gabe wanted to share his life with a woman. Not just any woman.

Gabe wanted the chance to share his life with Kayla, to get to know her and what made her happy and sad, laugh and cry. That she was pregnant should have sent him into a tailspin of denial, but it hadn't. He was excited that she was having a baby and he wanted to be there when she was born.

God, what was he thinking? He'd only known Kayla

three days and here he was thinking about happily ever after.

But that happily ever after would only be possible if Dakota and Kayla were safe. And at the moment, he feared they were both at the mercy of a killer.

He increased the pressure on the accelerator, fear pushing him faster than the road conditions warranted. Fear of losing two of the people he'd grown to love.

He couldn't let that happen.

No. He *wouldn't* let that happen.

Footsteps pounded on the stairs behind her as Kayla raced up the winding steps to the top of the tower. The lighthouse signal had long since been replaced by the automated beacon on a steel structure farther along the coast, but, thank God, the lighthouse was still enough of a local attraction for the staircase to be kept in good condition.

As she topped the winding staircase, she stumbled onto the level floor and crashed into metal railing rimming the center of the room where the beacon must once have stood.

Kayla felt her way around the wall to the opposite side. Darkness so thick she could taste it on her tongue pressed in on all sides. Blinded by the fog and complete nonexistence of light, she crouched against the stone wall on the farthest side of the walkway, as far away from the stairs as she could get. The vacant, glass-free windows gaped like open maws into the Devil's Shroud, their outlines barely visible in the abysmal gloom.

Tremors set in, shaking Kayla's body so badly her knees shook, threatening to buckle. Her arm ached and blood congealed on her hand. Bile rose in her throat, her stomach churning.

The only weapon she still carried was the can of wasp spray, her only defense against the man who'd attacked her before and nearly choked the life out of her. Out of desperation, she grabbed for the wrought-iron railing ringing the empty center where the beacon light once gleamed and pulled, praying the rust had done the trick, eating its way through the metal. But the railing remained sturdy, despite the gathering rust.

Armed with the wasp spray, she aimed it in the direction of the staircase, praying her aim would hold true and she wouldn't run out of juice in the can.

Light rose with the footsteps, closing in on her.

"Nancy!" Lawrence cried. "You can't leave me. You will never leave me."

The man had flipped. No amount of arguing would convince him Kayla wasn't Nancy. No amount of talking would make him back off. He wanted Nancy dead. Just as he'd wanted the other red-haired women who looked like her dead, each frightened beyond reason and then choked to their very last breath.

As light pierced the darkness, Kayla glanced around at the trap she'd gotten herself into. If she could lure him away from the top of the staircase long enough, she might be able to escape down the winding staircase and out into the night.

She waited, her breath caught in her throat, her body growing still. Falling apart wasn't an option. Her baby depended on her and she wanted to see Gabe again. She wanted to live, to know her child and to explore the blossoming relationship between herself and the cop. And Dakota needed more lessons in order to realize his full potential as an artist, and he could always use another friend to help him navigate his troubled teen years.

Kayla had far too many reasons to live to let one man extinguish her life. She crouched in a ready stance, waiting, gathering her breath and determination around her like a shield.

Lawrence lurched up the final step, breathing hard. The flashlight he carried bobbed crazily and then leveled, spanning the diameter of the room, sweeping left then right until it shone directly at her.

Kayla raised her hand to shield her vision from the beam, retaining what little night vision she could for when she plunged back down the dark stairs.

Lawrence's blood-red eyes squinted at her as though he had trouble seeing from the damage caused by the repellent. "Nancy," he moaned. "Why did you leave me?"

"I'm not Nancy," Kayla spoke in a calm, quiet voice, remaining crouched below the railing. Not that it would stop a bullet, but at least he couldn't see her any more clearly. If he wanted to kill her as he'd killed the others, he'd have to come around the room to get his hands on her.

"I just wanted to love you," he cried, tears slipping down his face.

"And you think choking someone is love?" she asked.

"I didn't mean to. You just wouldn't listen." He turned to the right, moving toward her one step at a time.

"I'm listening now." Kayla shifted, backing in the opposite direction. She needed him to come at least as far as she was from the door before she could make her lunge for freedom.

The ping of something hitting metal drew Kayla's attention to the stairwell behind Lawrence. Was someone climbing upward to her rescue? Could she hold off long enough?

Hope swelled in Kayla's breast until she remembered the gun Lawrence gripped in his hand. Anyone bursting through the doorway would be hailed with bullets, dead before they were any help to her, and all because she'd come to Cape Churn, bringing a killer with her.

Kayla wouldn't let that happen. The killing had to stop. No one else would die because of her.

One more step, take one more step, she wished silently.

"You're the only one I ever loved, don't you see?" He stepped closer, the gun rising.

"I don't see anything but a monster." Before Lawrence could level the weapon at her, she leaped to her feet and sprayed him square in the eyes with the wasp repellent, then leaped backward.

Lawrence dropped the flashlight and fired the gun, the bullet going wild, high into the air. He fired again. The flashlight rolled, the beam shining across at Kayla.

Kayla dived for the floor and low-crawled toward the stairs.

Footsteps pounded on the metal risers and Dakota exploded through the opening, flinging himself at Lawrence's back.

The blinded man roared, staggering forward, crashing headfirst into the wall.

"Run, Kayla, run!" Dakota shouted.

Had it just been her and Lawrence, she would have made a dive for the stairs, but she couldn't leave Dakota. If anything happened to him, she'd never forgive herself.

Lawrence fired off another round, the bullet singing past Kayla's ear. She scrambled around the railing, working her way toward Dakota.

Then Lawrence turned and slammed the boy into the wall, reared back, stumbled sideways and slammed backward again, only this time, the teen fell into the empty window well.

Dakota yelped, hanging out the window, his arms

locked around Lawrence's neck, his eyes wide with fear as he stared down at the rocky shore below.

Kayla reached out, her heart in her throat, praying for a miracle, too far away to help.

As Gabe pulled in to the driveway leading down to the lighthouse compound, he almost hit a figure running through the fog toward the cottage. He slammed on his brakes, lurching to a stop two feet from Jillian Taylor.

"Oh, dear God," she sobbed. "Gabe." She yanked open his door and yelled, "Help them. Please help them!"

Gabe grabbed a flashlight from the glove box, jumped out of the vehicle and gripped her arms. "Where is Kayla?"

"She was at the cottage. Lawrence shot at us. She shoved me out the door and told me to run and get help. I made it to the road, when Dakota rode up on his bicycle." Jillian dragged in several gasping breaths. "I heard shots, Gabe." Tears spilled down her cheeks. "They sounded like they came from farther away than the cottage. I think they're at the lighthouse. Hurry!" She shoved him, aiming him toward the lighthouse.

"Stay here and let the police units know where to go," Gabe called out over his shoulder.

Gabe ran toward the cottage, passing the black sedan Lawrence Wilson had driven the day he'd met Jillian at the bed-and-breakfast for dinner.

Dakota's bike lay flung to the ground in front of the porch.

His gut clenching tight, Gabe prayed he'd get to Kayla and Dakota in time. Another shot rang out, and he could hear someone shouting high above him.

His footsteps didn't falter as he sprinted down the narrow, worn path to the lighthouse, arriving at the splintered door as Kayla's scream pierced the fog, driving a jagged wedge into his heart.

He took the steps two at a time, climbing steadily upward, refusing to slow or stop to take a recovering breath. When he reached the top, his world skidded to a stop.

"Step back, cop, or I drop the boy on the rocks below," Lawrence warned.

Kayla stood with her right arm hanging limp at her side, clutching a spray can in her left hand. "He's got Dakota backed out a window. Don't provoke him."

"Let the boy go, Richard," Gabe said, forcing his voice into a low, calm tone, when all he wanted was to roar out his demand.

"All I want is Nancy," Richard said. "The boy for Nancy."

"She's dead," Gabe answered, knowing the man was delusional. "This woman isn't Nancy. You killed Nancy. This is Kayla."

"Give me Nancy or the boy dies." Richard brandished the pistol, his hand rising to the arms around his throat.

Kayla laid a hand on Gabe's arm. "Make the trade."

His heart stopped beating as he glanced at Kayla, pale and wounded, hunkered against the wall. "I can't let you do it."

"I won't be the cause of Dakota's death." Her fingers squeezed hard on his arm, the nails digging into the fabric of his shirt. "Make the trade."

"Hurry, I'm losing my grip on him." One hand held the teen's wrists, the other scrubbed across Richard's eyes as he blinked and squinted through swollen red lids.

"Don't believe him, Kayla," Dakota called out from outside the lighthouse window. "He's not going to drop me, because I'm not letting go."

"Then I'll throw myself out the window with the boy if Nancy doesn't go with me." Watson backed another step, shoving Dakota farther out the window. "The choice is clear. Nancy for the boy."

"I'm coming. Bring the boy back inside the window," Kayla called out.

Gabe grabbed for her arm, but she moved clear of him, working her way around toward Watson.

"Put down the gun or I won't come any farther," Kayla said, her voice firm and steady.

"No. You lie. You lied to me before. You cheated with that man when I trusted you."

"You have to trust me long enough to make the trade. Now, do it," she said, her voice soft but urgent.

"I'll kill you if you run. I'll shoot you dead." Lawrence aimed the pistol in Kayla's direction, his gaze wavering as though he couldn't really see her through his blistered eyes.

"Bring the boy in and I'll let you take me." She edged closer.

Lawrence hesitated then leaned forward.

As soon as Dakota cleared the window, he braced his feet on the ledge and pushed as hard as he could, sending Watson and himself flying forward into the wrought-iron railing at Kayla's feet.

Watson's gun hand hit the metal, knocking the weapon from his grasp. It skittered across the floor into the center of the ring of railing.

Dakota fell to the ground and rolled clear of Watson.

The killer grunted and reached out.

Before Gabe could get to Kayla, Watson had her by the ankle.

She twisted away from him, but the man clawed his way up her body and clamped an arm around her neck, holding her between him and Gabe. "Now you'll pay for hurting me. Just like the others."

"Let her go," Dakota cried out from behind, diving for the man.

Watson pushed Kayla toward the same window he'd almost dropped Gabe's son out of, his arm tightening around her throat.

Gabe quietly slipped up on one side of him. The man's eyes were swelling shut. He couldn't see Gabe as he approached.

In the illumination from the flashlight lying on the floor, Gabe signaled Dakota to come closer, hoping his son could distract the injured man long enough for Gabe to make a grab for Kayla.

Dakota cocked his leg and slammed a foot into Watson, sending him flying to the side, Kayla with him.

Watson's grip loosened to break his own fall.

Gabe caught Kayla in his arms and pushed her behind him.

The murderer roared, his face red with his fury, and he charged toward Gabe. Hunkering down like a linebacker, Gabe met him, absorbing the shock of his assault and sending him flying backward with a punch to the gut.

Watson staggered, righted himself and came back swinging wildly, his eyes swelled shut, his arms more or less flailing to find Gabe. "She's mine, damn you! Mine!"

Gabe ducked and landed a punch to the side of Watson's face. The man spun and steadied, swaying, obviously confused. He roared again and raced straight ahead, fists up, headed, not for Gabe and Kayla as he probably thought, but for the window.

"Lawrence, stop!" Kayla called out.

The man skidded, caught his foot on the uneven stone flooring and pitched forward through the gaping window.

Gabe and Kayla dived for him, but didn't get there in time to stop him from plunging to his death on the rocky shore two hundred feet below.

Kayla gasped and turned into Gabe's arms.

Dakota stood a few feet away, his eyes wide, his body shaking.

Gabe waved his hand, urging the teen closer.

Dakota stumbled toward them. When he got close enough, Gabe pulled him into his embrace with Kayla, his own body shaking with the aftershock of what could have happened.

"I almost lost you two," he whispered into Kayla's hair, squeezing Dakota's shoulder. "I can't tell you how much that scared me."

"Scared *you?*" Dakota laughed shakily. "You weren't the one hanging over the edge, facing a two-hundred-foot drop." His arm reached around Gabe's waist. "Thanks for being there for me."

"Thanks, Dakota, for coming to my rescue," Kayla said in a gravelly voice. She pulled back from Gabe and tugged the boy into her arms. "You're a very brave young man and I'm very much alive because of you." She hugged him close, staring over her shoulder at Gabe. "If you two hadn't come when you did…" She shook her head.

"I should have been here sooner." Gabe pulled her and Dakota back into his arms and crushed them to his chest, his eyes burning with tears. "I could have lost you both."

For a long moment they stood still in Gabe's embrace until a voice called out from the bottom of the stairwell.

"McGregor! You up there?"

Gabe chuckled and loosened his hold on the two people he loved.

Dakota straightened, the first to step back. "Guess we'd

better quit admiring the view and head back to the cottage."

"Yes, Chief. We're coming down," Gabe yelled into the stairwell. He turned toward Kayla.

She stood at one of the windows and smiled. "Look."

Gabe glanced out into the night. One by one, stars shone through the clearing fog, twinkling down at them as the mist dissipated and the heavens shone through.

"I guess the Devil's Shroud has lifted," Kayla commented. She leaned into Gabe.

His arm closed around her shoulders gently to avoid hurting her injury. "Come on, we need to get you to a hospital."

"Hey, Dad, would you show me that right hook sometime?" Dakota stood next to Gabe on the other side.

Gabe's chest swelled. Dakota had called him Dad. Rather than remark on his reference and embarrass the boy, Gabe played it cool, staring out at the night. "You bet, son."

"Let's go home." Kayla smiled at the two men.

Dakota bent to retrieve the flashlight. When he straightened, he asked, "The bed-and-breakfast?"

"No, the lighthouse cottage," Gabe and Kayla said in unison.

They laughed as they wound their way down the steps and stepped out into a clear, star-spangled night. Immediately, they were surrounded by police and emergency medical personnel, all demanding to know if they were all right, what had happened and where Lawrence Wilson— or, rather, Rick Watson—was.

Gabe insisted on Kayla seeing a doctor about her gunshot wound and to make sure the excitement and rough handling hadn't hurt her or the baby. Since he had a report to file, he told her he'd catch up with her at the hospital.

He loaded her into the back of an ambulance, sending Dakota with her to keep her safe, then he briefed the chief on all that had happened.

"Wilson, or Watson, had some very loose screws," the chief remarked. "At least he had the decency to die. Should save the taxpayers from the cost of a lengthy trial and imprisonment for life."

"Now the families of the victims can find closure for their lost loved ones and be relieved to know Watson won't hurt anyone else." Gabe wished Watson could have been stopped long before the other women had died. No one should have had to suffer the fear and pain he'd inflicted.

"We got word back that placed Watson in Seattle at the time of the gallery showing. He left a trail of credit card receipts. Should be no problem tying the deaths of the other red-haired victims to Richard Watson."

A chill slithered down Gabe's back at how close he'd come to losing Dakota and Kayla. "Sir, if you're done with me…"

"For now. Go on. I'm sure Kayla and Dakota could use a ride home from the hospital."

"Thanks." Gabe jogged for his SUV, running across Jillian on the way.

"Can you give me a ride back to town?" she asked.

"Sure, get in." Gabe held the door for her.

The normally neat business professional collapsed into the passenger seat. Black smudges of smeared mascara trailed down her cheeks, and her clothes were wrinkled and dirty. "I'm so sorry. I brought him out here."

"You didn't know what he was capable of."

She stared down at her muddy hands. "My stupidity could have gotten you all killed."

"It didn't. You helped me find them sooner by pointing me in the direction of the lighthouse."

Jillian glanced across the console at Gabe. "Can you ever forgive me?"

"Done." He buckled his seat belt and waited for Jillian to do the same.

Once she'd adjusted her strap, the real-estate agent leaned back against the leather seat, her breath catching on a sigh. "She's one lucky lady."

Gabe shifted into gear and pulled out onto the highway, headed for Cape Churn. "Who?"

"Kayla, silly." Jillian shot an exasperated frown at him.

"I know. She survived the night."

"Yeah, and she got you."

Gabe snorted. "How's that lucky?"

"You are the real deal. Someone who will never hurt her and always be there when she needs you." Jillian wiped a tear from her eye. "I hope I'll be half as lucky as she is and find someone like you."

"You'll find someone better, someone just right for you." Gabe chucked her chin with his fist. "You're not so bad yourself."

"Thanks, Gabe. Just don't wait too long to tell her that you love her. Life is way too short to miss a moment of being with the ones you love."

As they pulled in to town, the firefighters were rolling up their hoses and loading them onto their trucks. Most of the spectators had returned to their homes, the fire having been put out, nothing left of the station but rubble and smoldering embers.

"You can drop me off here." She nodded toward the firefighters. "I want to check on my office."

"Do you have a way home from there?"

"If my car escaped the flames, I can drive it home. Should be safe, now that you've taken care of the killer." She smiled. "Go. Kayla will be waiting for you. If you decide you two want to purchase the cottage, let me know. I'll make sure you get a great deal. It could be a great home for the three of you."

Gabe smiled as he drove toward the hospital. Three days were hardly long enough to know whether or not you were truly in love with a person, much less ready to buy a home together.

Yet, Jillian's words echoed in his mind. *Don't wait too long... Life is short...*

By the time he parked in the parking lot of the hospital, his blood was pumping and he couldn't wait for the engine to come to a complete stop before he was out of his SUV and jogging toward the emergency room.

A crowd filled the waiting room with firefighters, volunteers and citizens being checked for smoke inhalation and injuries.

Finally he found Emma Jenkins and pulled her aside.

"She's in exam room four," Emma said before he could ask. "The shoulder injury was only a flesh wound, requiring just a couple stitches."

"Is she all right?"

Emma patted his shoulder. "She'll be fine."

"The baby?"

A grin spread across her face. "Her heart is beating like a bass drum and she was kicking like a soccer player."

"Her?" Gabe's heart swelled, his eyes misting.

"Yeah. We went ahead and performed a sonogram to make sure everything was where it should be. No dangly parts on that kid. It's a girl." She clamped a hand over her mouth. "Sorry, I'm not supposed to share that information. Act surprised when she tells you. Oh, and remember, she and I have rescheduled our lunch date for tomorrow at the marina. I could use a new friend."

Gabe's chest swelled with so much love he could hardly walk straight. He dodged nurses, empty wheelchairs and emergency medical technicians on his way to room four. Inside, Dakota stood beside the bed, smiling at Kayla as she sat with her legs hanging over the side.

When he walked in, they both turned toward him.

"About time," Dakota remarked. "We're hungry and ready to go."

"Hungry? Sounds like *you're* the only hungry one." Gabe clapped a hand on his son's back and faced Kayla.

Looking into her deep green eyes, he felt as if he'd been sucker punched full-on in the gut. This woman was the one for him. From her deep auburn hair, porcelain skin and green eyes to her great big heart.

"Did you know Kayla's going to have a baby?" Dakota asked. "I've always wanted a sister to torment. It's a girl."

Gabe smiled down at Kayla. "Is that so?"

Kayla's lips twisted into a wry grin. "Emma told you, didn't she?"

He nodded. "Can't keep secrets for long in Cape Churn."

"The nurse has some paperwork for Kayla to fill out. It'll be another fifteen minutes before we're out of here." Dakota's eyes rolled to the ceiling, a smile tugging at his lips. "And I'm sure you two are about to start kissing or something."

"You think?" Gabe asked, his attention on Kayla's lips, not his son. The boy had the right idea.

"Come on, Dad, I'm not a kid." He held out his hand. "If you have some change for the vending machine, I'll make myself scarce."

Gabe fished in his pocket and dumped a wad of change into Dakota's hand. "Go for it."

"Thanks, Dad." Dakota dived for the door, his stomach rumbling loudly. "Told you I was hungry," he yelled from the hall.

Kayla laughed, her gaze following Dakota. "He's a good kid."

"He was right, you know."

"About what?" When her eyes met his, her chin dipped and a blush blossomed in her cheeks as she fiddled with the hem of her shirt.

"There's gonna be some kissing or something going on in here." He reached out and tipped her chin up. "Starting about now." Bending forward, he brushed his lips across hers.

Her good hand rested on his chest and then pushed away. "Are you sure this is what you want? You didn't seem so sure the other night."

"I was as soon as I left you."

"How do I know you won't leave again?"

He smiled. "Because I can't."

Kayla's brows furrowed. "Why not?"

"I've fallen in love with a beautiful redhead."

"So soon?" Her brows lifted into her tumbled curls. "I didn't think you believed in true love."

"It only took the right woman to prove me wrong."

Her lips parted on a quickly indrawn breath. "How am I supposed to be serious when you say such nice things to me?"

"I'm serious enough for the both of us." He pulled her into his arms. "Let me prove it to you." Gabe claimed her mouth, pressing her body against his, the rise of his erection nudging her tummy. When he lifted his head, her eyes were glazed.

"I think it will take a lot more than that to prove it to me." Kayla curled her fingers around the back of his neck and brought his mouth back to hers.

"Baby, time is on our side," he whispered. "We have the rest of our lives."

* * * * *

SUSPENSE

COMING NEXT MONTH
AVAILABLE MARCH 27, 2012

#1699 CAVANAUGH'S BODYGUARD
Cavanaugh Justice
Marie Ferrarella

#1700 LAWMAN'S PERFECT SURRENDER
Perfect, Wyoming
Jennifer Morey

#1701 GUARDIAN IN DISGUISE
Conard County: The Next Generation
Rachel Lee

#1702 TEXAS BABY SANCTUARY
Chance, Texas
Linda Conrad

REQUEST YOUR FREE BOOKS!
2 FREE NOVELS PLUS 2 FREE GIFTS!

ROMANTIC
SUSPENSE

Sparked by Danger, Fueled by Passion.

YES! Please send me 2 FREE Harlequin® Romantic Suspense novels and my 2 FREE gifts (gifts are worth about $10). After receiving them, if I don't wish to receive any more books, I can return the shipping statement marked "cancel." If I don't cancel, I will receive 4 brand-new novels every month and be billed just $4.49 per book in the U.S. or $5.24 per book in Canada. That's a saving of at least 14% off the cover price! It's quite a bargain! Shipping and handling is just 50¢ per book in the U.S. and 75¢ per book in Canada.* I understand that accepting the 2 free books and gifts places me under no obligation to buy anything. I can always return a shipment and cancel at any time. Even if I never buy another book, the two free books and gifts are mine to keep forever.

240/340 HDN FEFR

Name	(PLEASE PRINT)	
Address		Apt. #
City	State/Prov.	Zip/Postal Code

Signature (if under 18, a parent or guardian must sign)

Mail to the Reader Service:
IN U.S.A.: P.O. Box 1867, Buffalo, NY 14240-1867
IN CANADA: P.O. Box 609, Fort Erie, Ontario L2A 5X3

Not valid for current subscribers to Harlequin Romantic Suspense books.

Want to try two free books from another line?
Call 1-800-873-8635 or visit www.ReaderService.com.

* Terms and prices subject to change without notice. Prices do not include applicable taxes. Sales tax applicable in N.Y. Canadian residents will be charged applicable taxes. Offer not valid in Quebec. This offer is limited to one order per household. All orders subject to credit approval. Credit or debit balances in a customer's account(s) may be offset by any other outstanding balance owed by or to the customer. Please allow 4 to 6 weeks for delivery. Offer available while quantities last.

Your Privacy—The Reader Service is committed to protecting your privacy. Our Privacy Policy is available online at www.ReaderService.com or upon request from the Reader Service.

We make a portion of our mailing list available to reputable third parties that offer products we believe may interest you. If you prefer that we not exchange your name with third parties, or if you wish to clarify or modify your communication preferences, please visit us at www.ReaderService.com/consumerschoice or write to us at Reader Service Preference Service, P.O. Box 9062, Buffalo, NY 14269. Include your complete name and address.

HRS11B

Harlequin®

ROMANTIC
SUSPENSE

Danger is hot on their heels!

Catch the thrill with author

LINDA CONRAD

Chance, Texas

Sam Chance, a U.S. marshal in the Witness Security
Service, is sworn to protect Grace Brown and her
one-year-old son after Grace testifies against an infamous
drug lord and he swears revenge. With Grace on the edge of
fleeing, Sam knows there is only one safe place he can take
her—home. But when the danger draws near, it's not just
Sam's life on the line but his heart, too.

Watch out for

Texas Baby Sanctuary
Available April 2012

Texas Manhunt
Available May 2012

www.Harlequin.com

*Taft Bowman knew he'd ruined any chance he'd had
for happiness with Laura Pendleton when he drove her
away years ago…and into the arms of another man,
thousands of miles away. Now she was back, a widow
with two small children…and despite himself, he was
starting to believe in second chances.*

Harlequin Special® Edition® presents a new installment
in USA TODAY bestselling author
RaeAnne Thayne's miniseries,
THE COWBOYS OF COLD CREEK.

*Enjoy a sneak peek of
A COLD CREEK REUNION*

Available April 2012 from Harlequin® Special Edition®

A younger woman stood there, and from this distance he
had only a strange impression, as though she was somehow standing on an island of calm amid the chaos of the
scene, the flashing lights of the emergency vehicles, shouts
between his crew members, the excited buzz of the crowd.

And then the woman turned and he just about tripped
over a snaking fire hose somebody shouldn't have left
there.

Laura.

He froze, and for the first time in fifteen years as a fire-
fighter, he forgot about the incident, his mission, just what
the hell he was doing here.

Laura.

Ten years. He hadn't seen her in all that time, since
the week before their wedding when she had given him
back his ring and left town. Not just town. She had left the
whole damn country, as if she couldn't run far enough to

get away from him.

Some part of him desperately wanted to think he had made some kind of mistake. It couldn't be her. That was just some other slender woman with a long sweep of honey-blond hair and big, blue, unforgettable eyes. But no. It was definitely Laura. Sweet and lovely.

Not his.

He was going to have to go over there and talk to her. He didn't want to. He wanted to stand there and pretend he hadn't seen her. But he was the fire chief. He couldn't hide out just because he had a painful history with the daughter of the property owner.

Sometimes he hated his job.

Will Taft and Laura be able to make the years recede...or is the gulf between them too broad to ever cross?

Find out in
A COLD CREEK REUNION
Available April 2012 from Harlequin® Special Edition®
wherever books are sold.

Celebrate the 30th anniversary
of Harlequin® Special Edition® with a bonus story
included in each Special Edition® book in April!